"We were so young," Frannie whispered. "What we were feeling wasn't real. It would never have worked."

"Maybe, maybe not. Maybe this is all about another chance."

"How can we have another chance? I'm not the same person I was. Neither are you."

"You think so?" Roberto murmured. "Let's find out."

And he leaned in to press his mouth to hers.

Nearly two decades had passed and she'd forgotten a million and one things in that time. But she remembered his kisses, oh, she remembered his kisses.

Dear Reader,

"If I have seen further it is by standing on the shoulders of giants," Sir Isaac Newton famously said. In writing the wrap-up book for the latest Fortune family continuity, THE FORTUNES OF TEXAS: RETURN TO RED ROCK, I've definitely stood on the shoulders of giants. The sixty-plus books that are part of the various Fortunes continuities feature a host of bestselling and award-winning authors, as well as a collection of beloved characters. Tall order, then, to step in and add my bit to the whole, but we're very excited about the Return to Red Rock continuity. We've got excitement, mystery, a dash of intrigue, a hint of danger and a generous helping of happily-ever-after. So pour yourself a cool drink, shut off the phone and curl up on the couch with us as the latest Fortunes find love.

As always, I'd love to hear what you think at kristin@kristinhardy.com. Stop by www.kristinhardy.com for news, recipes and contests, or to sign up for my newsletter to be informed of new releases.

Enjoy!

Kristin Hardy

A FORTUNE WEDDING

KRISTIN HARDY

SPECIAL EDITION

Published by Silhouette Books

America's Publisher of Contemporary Romance

Special thanks and acknowledgment to Kristin Hardy
for her contribution to the
Fortunes of Texas: Return to Red Rock miniseries.

SILHOUETTE BOOKS

ISBN-13: 978-0-373-65458-1

A FORTUNE WEDDING

Recycling programs
for this product may
not exist in your area.

Visit Silhouette Books at www.eHarlequin.com

Printed in U.S.A.

Books by Kristin Hardy

Silhouette Special Edition

††*Where There's Smoke* #1720
††*Under the Mistletoe* #1725
††*Vermont Valentine* #1739
††*Under His Spell* #1786
***Always a Bridesmaid* #1832
Her Christmas Surprise #1871
‡‡*The Chef's Choice* #1919
††*Always Valentine's Day* #1952
~*A Fortune Wedding* #1976

Harlequin Blaze

My Sexiest Mistake #44
*Scoring #78
*As Bad As Can Be #86
**Slippery When Wet* #94
†*Turn Me On* #148
†*Cutting Loose* #156
†*Nothing but the Best* #164
§*Certified Male* #187
§*U.S. Male* #199
Caught #242
Bad Influence #295
Hot Moves #307
Bad Behavior #319

††Holiday Hearts
**Logan's Legacy Revisited
‡‡The McBains of Grace Harbor
*Under the Covers
†Sex & the Supper Club
§Sealed with a Kiss
~Fortunes of Texas: Return to Red Rock

KRISTIN HARDY

has always wanted to write, starting her first novel while still in grade school. Although she became a laser engineer by training, she never gave up her dream of being an author. In 2002, her first completed manuscript, *My Sexiest Mistake,* debuted in Harlequin's Blaze line; it was subsequently made into a movie by the Oxygen network. Kristin lives in New Hampshire with her husband and collaborator. Check out her Web site at www.kristinhardy.com.

To Susan, for her patience and careful editing.
To the other Fortunes of Texas authors
for being great collaborators.
And to Stephen,
who's been my best fortune yet.

Acknowledgments

Thanks go to
William Hartley of the Hartley Law Firm and
Lt. Ron Marquis of the Boerne, Texas Police Department
for helping bring this story to life.
Any errors are mine.

Prologue

"Come on, boy, come on," Roberto Mendoza muttered, crouching over the withers of Cisco, his big bay gelding, as they raced up the tree-studded grassy slope. The speed was intoxicating. The wind rushed over his skin. A kaleidoscope of sound filled his ears—the thud of hoofbeats, the rush of his own breath.

The silvery sound of laughter ahead of him.

And then they burst up onto the hilltop, the great blue bowl of the sky arching overhead.

"Hah! We beat you!" Frannie Fortune whooped, reining in her little chestnut mare and wheeling around. "Who says the girls can't outdo the boys?" With her short, sunbeam-blond hair and tilted eyes, she looked like a pixie, ready for mischief.

Life, Roberto thought, just didn't get any better than this.

"You girls only won because you took a shortcut," he told her.

"Don't blame us because we're smarter. We just took a faster way."

"Yeah, like straight up the side of the hill."

"Admit it, you're impressed."

He grinned. "I am, but next time you decide to take your shortcut, leave me with a suicide note for your uncle. I'm supposed to be watching out for you."

Her cheeks were still flushed with the excitement of the race. "I keep telling Uncle Ryan I don't need looking after. So I got thrown once. It can happen to anyone. You try staying in the saddle when a killdeer flies up between the feet of that monster you're on," she challenged. "See how you feel when your fanny hits the ground."

Roberto's lips twitched as he slid off Cisco. "I guess you'll have to come to my rescue."

"If you're lucky." She gave him an arch look.

How had he ever thought her standoffish? It hadn't been that, but simple shyness that had kept her quiet and to herself when she'd first arrived at the Double Crown Ranch where he worked. As the weeks had passed, she'd blossomed, quiet diffidence giving way to a sly humor that perpetually hovered around that delicate mouth, the surprisingly bawdy laughter that burst out of her more and more often as the days went by.

Maybe it was just being here, out on the ranch, amid the rolling terrain of Texas hill country. It could make anybody happy, although he might be biased. No matter where his life took him, Roberto thought, no place would ever feel as right as this patch of territory where he knew nearly every tree, bush and bird by name. It was in his blood, as much a part of him as his brown eyes.

Frannie walked over to stand next to him. "You think you'll ever leave here?" she asked, as if she knew what he'd been thinking.

He watched as she bent down to pick a long stalk of grass. "I'd have to have a real good reason. I figure I'll save my money, buy a place of my own someday."

Living and working out on the land, he couldn't imagine anything better. Certainly not sitting all day in a college classroom, no matter how much his father wanted him to. José Mendoza hadn't taken the news of his twenty-year-old son dropping out well. To avoid skull fractures from the two of them butting heads in the family's restaurant, Red, Roberto had come to work at the Double Crown, where his uncle Ruben Mendoza ran operations for the Fortune family.

And where the lovely, coltish Frannie had appeared for a visit just days later.

Too bad she'd somehow gotten snowed into dating Lloyd Fredericks, the original self-important, silver-spoon guy. But she was a Fortune and he was a Fredericks, so maybe they did belong together. It still set Roberto's teeth on edge every time he saw Fredericks drive in to pick her up. The jerk didn't deserve a woman like Frannie.

"So, what are you going to call your ranch?" Frannie interrupted his thoughts. "The Rocking RM? The Double R?"

"I was thinking Red Oaks."

"How about the Slowpoke?" she offered.

His eyes narrowed. "Remind me again who won when we raced last week?"

"That's because you had an unfair advantage," she argued. "Cisco's two hands taller than Peaches. We had to outsmart you."

What she'd done was about stop his heart when he'd seen her tearing up the side of the hill. She might have started out quiet and shy, but she was fearless now.

"You just got lucky this time," he said.

"No, I was prepared," Frannie corrected him, twirling her grass. "Lloyd says that's what luck is, just opportunity meeting preparation."

"That sounds like your boyfriend. Always looking for an angle."

She rolled her eyes. "He's not my boyfriend. We're just going out. Anyway, I don't want to talk about Lloyd. You buy Red Oaks and I'll come to visit." She gave him an impish look. "And Peaches and I will beat you then, too."

He reached out and swiped the blade of grass from her hand.

"Hey," she protested.

"You need to learn some respect for your elders."

"My elders?" She snorted. "You think a fancy new hat makes you all grown-up?" That all-too-delectable mouth of hers curved.

Roberto eyed her. "You got a problem with my hat?"

"I don't know, but maybe you do." And quick as a flash, she swiped the black Stetson and dashed away, squealing.

He sprinted after her. "Oh, you're gonna be sorry."

"Big talk," she scoffed, clapping the hat on top of her

head. She was willow thin and fleet, feinting one direction and dashing the other, making him give chase until both of them were laughing and out of breath, circling the red oak that crowned the top of the hill.

"Give it up," he told her as they faced off on either side of a stand of piñon.

She glanced over to Peaches as though judging her distance. "Not a chance." She faked one way and he mirrored her, faked the other. And then she went just a fraction too far and he whipped around the tree and caught her, snaking an arm around her waist to draw her in.

"That's it, *chica,* you're in for it now," he growled.

"Oh, yeah? What are you going to do to me?" There was humor in those soft blue eyes, and mischief and glee. And under it all, something else, something that started the blood rushing in his veins. He caught a hint of scent that made him think of spring and sunshine. He could feel every breath she took. His pulse thundered in his ears.

She wasn't even out of school yet, he reminded himself. He worked for her uncle. He had no business kissing her. Even as his lips hovered over hers, he made himself release her.

And then Frannie leaned in to press her sweet, warm mouth to his.

Chapter One

Red Rock, Texas
May 2009
Three days after the Spring Fling…

How in the name of God had it happened? Frannie Fredericks wondered as she stared through the visitor's window in the Red Rock County Jail. One minute she'd been riding horses that golden summer, the next she'd been pregnant, the next, married.

And the next, she'd been bent over her husband's dead body at the town's Spring Fling, the blood on her hands black in the moonlight.

Suspicion had slid into interrogation, and, impossibly, arrest, the giddy shrieks of the kids on the carnival rides fifty yards away still ringing in her ears. And now, she was here in the county jail on the wrong side of the barrier, accused of Lloyd Fredericks' murder.

Lily Fortune, Frannie's sort-of aunt, sat as calm and poised as an aristocrat, her dark hair up in a twist, her hand holding the black telephone receiver that linked them. From the rows of windows to either side they heard angry accusations, plaintive whispers, false bravado as people visited sons and daughters, spouses, lovers, friends. The temperature in the room rose with the closely packed bodies.

"You really don't have to come here," Frannie said into the handset.

Lily gave a serene smile. "Of course I do. You forget, I know what it's like."

Almost ten years before, Lily had been the one behind bars, wrongly accused of the murder of Ryan Fortune's then wife. She'd been freed, though, freed to finally marry Ryan, her lifelong love, freed to find happiness.

Frannie could barely remember what happiness felt like. "How did you make it through?" she asked, her voice barely audible.

"I knew I was innocent. The same way you're innocent. Of course, it would help matters if you told that to someone. Or if you told them anything else that you know."

Anything else that you know. Frannie looked down at the floor. "My lawyer said we shouldn't talk about the case."

Lily was silent for a long moment, then let out a quiet sigh. "All right. We're behind you, Frannie, whatever you decide. And we're doing our best to get you out of here. That DA makes me so mad, holding you without bail as a campaign stunt. We'll have you out of here soon, though. William's working on it."

William Fortune, Frannie's uncle. Something flickered in Lily's eyes when she said his name, a light that had been missing in the four years since she'd lost Ryan to cancer. Frannie's life might have been in turmoil, the lives of all of the Fortunes of late, but at least one good thing had come of it.

"You like him, don't you?"

"Well, of course," Lily answered too quickly. "He's been very helpful since he came out from California."

"I don't think it has anything to do with being helpful," Frannie countered. "And you're blushing."

Lily straightened. "I am not. It's just warm in here."

For the first time since that nightmare moment of discovering Lloyd's body, Frannie found herself smiling. "You've always been so good to me," she said.

"You make it easy."

The two women had hit it off from the day they'd met, despite the twenty-five-year difference in their ages. Maybe it was that they were both outsiders of a sort—Lily because she'd just married into the Fortune family and Frannie because, well, the children of a family's black sheep always were.

Growing up, all Frannie had ever wanted was a normal life—a home instead of a succession of apartments and hotels, a father instead of a parade of uncles. She would have traded anything she had for a stable, loving mother. Instead, she and her brothers had been stuck with the brash, temperamental, self-destructive Cindy Fortune, which had been better than being raised by wolves, but only marginally. Cindy operated on three levels: derision, manipulation and indifference.

She'd been working on husband number five when a few too many drinks and some ill-advised behavior had wrecked it. Short on money—her trust fund was long gone—she'd had to go to plan B. For housing, a stay on a yacht in the Mediterranean with some of her jet-setting friends. And if she couldn't marry for money herself, she'd marry her daughter off, instead. So she'd dumped seventeen-year-old Frannie with Ryan and the rest of the Fortunes at the Double Crown, taking care to introduce her to the wealthy Fredericks family and their eligible son before heading out to Santorini.

How strange it had been to be with people who didn't make a lifestyle of making scenes, Frannie remembered. Adults who were responsible. Cindy might have infuriated and appalled them, but they never gave a hint of it to Frannie, just loved her and encouraged her and gave her the space to discover who she really was.

"Cindy dropped me at the ranch like extra baggage." Frannie shook her head. "No one ever said anything, not Uncle Kingston, not Uncle Ryan."

Lily frowned. "You weren't extra baggage, you were family. Kingston offered to let you stay from the time you were a toddler, you know."

"What?" Startled, Frannie stared at her.

"Every time Cindy showed up angling for money and talking about what a burden motherhood was, he'd offer to take you, all of you kids. When you were about five, Kingston demanded that she let him adopt the lot of you." Lily looked down. "She said no, of course. Ryan said it was the worst fight they'd ever had."

"I had no idea. She never said…"

"She wouldn't, would she?" Lily put her hand to the clear barrier between them. "Frannie, you're dear to all of us and we all want you out of here. Whatever you think it's doing to help your case by staying quiet, you're wrong. Don't make a mistake that you're going to pay for forever."

But she already had—that long-ago summer when Lloyd Fredericks had come around flirting. Lloyd had been a junior at Rice University, sophisticated and handsome and initially irresistible.

Until she'd gotten to know Roberto Mendoza, the dark-eyed ranch hand with the smile that flashed like hidden treasure. She'd lost her heart. He'd walked away.

And then things had changed shockingly quickly. One moment she'd had all the possibilities in the world. The next, only a single option had remained—a night's misjudgment becoming a life choice. The years had gone by, her world shrinking around her until she no longer recognized that girl she'd been. And now she was here, accused of Lloyd's murder, unable to deny it.

Unable to even bring herself to think about the alternative—that the one who really belonged in the cell might be Josh, their son.

Roberto Mendoza stood in the afternoon sunlight of the empty field, watching a line of ants weave a path through the grass. Ticket stubs and bits of litter fluttered in the breeze, scudding along to catch around the bottoms of the row of honey mesquite that lined the field's edge. They were almost finished blooming now, showering the grass with their pale yellow petals and infusing the air with a faint hint of sweetness. It was the scent that always made him think of home.

He shook his head. How the hell had he wound up back in Red Rock? Eighteen years before, he'd started walking away and just kept going. Time was, he'd figured it would take an act of God or a funeral to get him home. In the end, it had only taken one phone call, a call he'd been powerless to ignore. His family needed him, it had been that simple. And he, who had resisted all ties for so long, started the long drive back.

He'd figured it would be quick and over; he'd hit town planning on it. He'd figure out who was threatening his family and put an end to it. He'd never expected to be sucked into the middle of someone else's mess.

Or that he'd be powerless to walk away.

At the sound of an engine, Roberto turned to see a dark blue sedan pull off the highway and crunch down the gravel road to park beside his truck. The doors opened and two men got out. He didn't move, just watched as they adjusted their jackets and walked over to him, taking their time. They came to a stop before him.

"I guess you'd be Roberto Mendoza," said the older of the two. He was heavyset with thinning, brownish hair, but the man who made the mistake of thinking he was soft was the one who'd wind up on the losing end of the fight.

Roberto nodded. "And you'd be...?"

He flipped out his badge in a practiced motion. "Lieutenant Len Wheeler, Red Rock PD. This here's Investigator Bobby McCaskill. How about you show us some ID?"

Roberto's brow rose as he brought out his wallet. "You always card citizens offering information?"

Wheeler glanced up from the driver's license. "The job's about paying attention to details," he said mildly, and handed Roberto's license back. "Now, how about you tell us why we're here?"

"There's something I think you need to see."

Wheeler's washed-out blue eyes studied him. "I checked the files. The units on the scene interviewed you the night of Fredericks' murder. Said you reported an unspecified person dressed in a black hoodie walking away from the scene."

"Black and red. Maybe."

"Whatever this thing is, why didn't you tell the on-site officers then, when the scene was fresh?"

"It wasn't until I was running it over in my mind later that I realized there was something else that might have mattered."

"And you couldn't just call it into the hotline?" McCaskill asked sourly.

Roberto shot him a glance. "I left a message on the hotline a week and a half ago." A week and a half. A week and a half that Frannie had been sitting in the county jail for Lloyd Fredericks' murder when he knew damned well she was innocent.

And no matter how little he thought of the faithless woman she'd proven to be, he couldn't leave the golden, laughing girl from the hilltop to that. "You didn't do anything the tip. I figured I needed to take things into my own hands," he said aloud. Clear his conscience and be done with it.

Wheeler shook his head. "We got ourselves a good

two hundred pages of notes from that fool hotline. Something about the murder of a guy like Fredericks brings out all the bedbugs."

Like you, was the unspoken subtext. Roberto's jaw tightened. "Do you want to solve this case?"

"Already have." Wheeler smiled. "We got us a guy calls every day swearing Ronald Reagan appeared in his bedroom to tell him Dr. Phil did it. Another one who says it was all a plot by the arugula-eating elitists." Abruptly, the smile vanished. "You live in Denver. Long way from Red Rock. You mind telling us what you were doing in town and all the way down here that night?"

It shouldn't have taken him by surprise. It did. "I was at the Spring Fling."

"Spring Fling was going on a good twenty, thirty yards away from here." Wheeler glanced around. "This area would have been back away from the booths, out in the dark. So maybe you want to explain just how it was you happened to be around to see your mysterious person. And there was a whole line of outhouses over by the dance, and in the opinion of our officers you were stone-cold sober when they talked to you, so if I was you, I'd think twice about wasting our time with any stories about needing a bathroom." And that quickly, the affable exterior fell away to show the cop beneath.

Whether or not to tell the truth was an easy decision. Figuring out how much to tell was harder. "I came back from Denver for family reasons."

"That's right, someone burned up your dad's restaurant." That was McCaskill, reaching down to pluck a ticket stub off the ground. "I guess they didn't like their combination platter."

It was a clumsy attempt to provoke a reaction. Roberto wasn't about to rise to it. "You've been doing your homework."

"Yep, we've done a lot of studying." Wheeler squinted at the trees. "Funny thing, the Fortunes have been having their share of fire trouble, too. What was that note Lily Fortune got? 'This one wasn't an accident, either'? You know anything about that?"

"Why would you think I would?" Or about the other cryptic notes—*One of the Fortunes is not who you think.*

"Oh, maybe on account of you worked at the ranch about twenty years back."

Roberto shot him a look. "You investigating the murder of Lloyd Fredericks or you investigating me?"

"Lloyd Fredericks. Although you're becoming an interesting sideline. So what were you doing creeping around back here, Mendoza?"

Funny how sometimes your entire life could hinge on chance. He hadn't planned to attend the Spring Fling, wouldn't have.

Except for the message.

"I got a call to meet someone. They said they had some information for me."

"What was it?"

Roberto shrugged. "I never saw them." The caller hadn't bothered to show up. Instead, Lloyd Fredericks had.

McCaskill flipped the ticket stub away. "No mystery caller, just you standing here when Lloyd Fredericks got his head staved in twenty yards away. Oh, and your imaginary hooded avenger running away—"

"Walking."

"Yeah, sure, walking away. Except no one else around here saw them. You really expect us to buy that?"

"Take it easy, Bobby," Wheeler said. "Who was it you were supposed to meet?"

"I don't know."

"Man? Woman?"

"I don't know," Roberto repeated. "It was a cell phone message, a bad connection with a lot of noise in the background. Look," he snapped, patience finally evaporating. "I came here to show you something that could be important to your investigation, not get grilled. You got any more questions to ask, I want a lawyer."

Wheeler looked mild again. "No need to lawyer up, we're just talking here. Why don't you show us whatever it is that's got you so excited?"

"Over there." Roberto pointed over at the line of bushes at the field's edge. "I told your officers about the guy hurrying off a couple of minutes before the screaming started. I wasn't watching all that close, just figured he was swinging his arms, but the way he was swinging them was funny. I got to thinking maybe he tossed something away. That's why I called the hotline. I figured you'd check it out, but you all seemed a lot more interested in railroading Frannie Fredericks."

Wheeler looked interested. "You got some kind of acquaintance with Miz Fredericks? Or the deceased?"

Roberto cursed himself silently. "I told you, no more questions without a lawyer. And if you don't look in that honey mesquite over there in the next two minutes, I'm going to fish the damned thing out and haul it to the lab myself."

"Now you just take it easy, Mr. Mendoza." Even as Wheeler said the words, McCaskill crossed to where Roberto pointed.

Roberto could tell the minute he saw it, see the sudden attention in the line of his body. "Hey, Len, you might want to come on over here."

Wheeler had been on the job too long to show obvious interest in anything, but he moved with purpose to stare at what Roberto had found.

It had been tossed back into the center of a thicket of branches, a thick metal bar maybe the length of a man's forearm, but far more deadly. And Roberto knew what they'd see if they looked closer—the dark residue, the clots of matter. And hair.

"Bobby, get the forensics team out here," Wheeler said without looking up.

"Already got 'em on the line." He spoke into the phone as Wheeler bent back the twigs under the end of the bar with a pen.

"When did you find this, Mr. Mendoza?"

"This morning, after I got sick and tired of waiting for one of you people to call me back or at least get your asses out here."

"And you haven't touched it?"

The mildness was gone, the gaze flat and assessing.

"I think I want that lawyer, now," Roberto said.

"We'll set you up with your phone call as soon as we get back to the station," Wheeler said as he and McCaskill fell in on either side of Roberto.

He felt a thread of disquiet. "Are you arresting me?"

"Just taking you in for some questions. Because I've got a lot more of them for you. Starting with why we found pictures of someone who looks a whole lot like you on Lloyd Fredericks' cell phone."

Wrought-iron chandeliers cast golden light over the tiled floor. Antique serapes hung on pale ocher walls next to antique maps of Texas. In three or four hours, the main room of Red would be filled with diners, noise and the savory scents of the restaurant's Tex-Mex specialties. At this hour, though, it was still peaceful and empty.

Sort of. "It's a good thing you own a restaurant, otherwise the rehearsal dinner would break you," Jane Gilliam commented, glancing around the polished wood table at the people who had become a kind of second family to her in a matter of months.

And at the man who'd come to mean everything.

Jorge Mendoza had the knife-edged cheekbones and the rogue's grin of a heartbreaker, but when he looked at her, there was something more, something deep and true for her alone. Impossible to think that mere months before she'd barely been aware of his existence. Now, he was her first thought upon rising and her last before going to sleep.

And soon, he would be her husband.

Catching her gaze, he leaned over to kiss her thoroughly.

For a moment, Jane just sank into it before realizing the impropriety. "Hey," she said. "There are people here."

"They're not people, they're family," he corrected, giving her another kiss for good measure. "Besides, they're used to it."

"He's right, you know," José Mendoza said, planting a kiss on his wife, Maria.

"Pay attention, you." Maria pushed him away, round cheeks tinting.

He stroked his graying mustache. "I am paying attention."

"We have a rehearsal dinner to plan," she scolded. "We barely have two months until the wedding."

"It's all right, I know the owner," said José.

"Who is going to be very embarrassed if his son's rehearsal dinner is a failure," she responded starchily.

"Women," José said to Jorge, shaking his head.

"They never have their priorities straight," Jorge agreed.

"Listen to Mama," admonished his sister Christina. "We have to get your dinner planned."

"And the wedding planned and the honeymoon planned. Plan, plan plan. Life doesn't always have to be serious," Jorge reminded her.

"Trust me, I know." Her mouth curved as she watched a girl run past, followed by a giggling boy of about four. "That's why you plan, so you can afford to not be serious. Bowie, stop barging around after Elsa or you'll break something," she ordered.

"Like your head," added Sierra, Jorge's youngest sister, as she tied up her waist-length, curly brown hair. "Come on, Jorge, let's get the planning done so we can go out into the courtyard and have some dinner."

"You've gotten bossier since you've become a mother," he observed, watching her pull her daughter onto her lap.

"I was always bossy," she countered. "Anyway, think of Jane."

"Oh, trust me, I do," he assured her. "In fact I—" A snatch of electronic music played and he pulled out his cell phone, glancing at the display before opening it up. "About time you called. Everybody's here, you're the only one missing. Now get your lazy—what?" He stopped. "You're *where?*" The grin disappeared in an instant, replaced by shock and then a taut anxiety. "Whoa. Wait a minute, hold on. Run through it from the beginning." Jorge listened, then cursed. "They're out of their minds. How can they—all right, all right. Don't worry about it, I'll take care of it. Give me fifteen minutes, thirty tops." He ended the call and lowered the phone slowly to the table.

"What? What is it?" Jane asked.

Jorge stared into space for a moment, then stirred. "That was Roberto."

"Where is he?" Worry infused Maria's voice. "He's more than an hour late."

"He's at the police department." Jorge looked at them all helplessly. "They're holding him for questioning in the murder of Lloyd Fredericks."

Chapter Two

"Cordell Fredericks conducted the reading of the will last week, but the bulk of Lloyd's property is held in your living trust. That means it's all yours." Royce Gahan glanced up from the papers on his polished mahogany desk to Frannie, sitting across from him.

It was all faintly unreal, going from orange jumpsuits at the county jail to a plush leather client chair at the office of their lawyer. Her lawyer, now. One minute she'd been in a cell, the next she'd been released on her own recognizance.

At least until the police changed their minds.

"Was there anything in the will I should know about?"

"I don't think so. Just the disposal of some Fredericks family heirlooms. There's a copy of the document in the folder I've given you. It's…unfortunate you couldn't be there."

Frannie didn't think so. She was happy to have missed it. Even without the suspicion cast on her, the reading would have been unpleasant. Jillian Fredericks had never made any secret of the fact that she thought Frannie had trapped Lloyd. Never mind that Frannie's trust fund had largely supported them, that he was just as much at fault as she for the unplanned pregnancy.

Or more.

When Frannie had turned up pregnant after leaving Texas, Cindy had dragged her back to Red Rock to face Lloyd. It had taken a DNA test to convince the Fredericks family. By that time, Frannie had been so emotionally shell-shocked that she'd been in no shape to decide anything. Lloyd will take care of you, Cindy had told her, and she'd obeyed.

Why he'd married her, Frannie couldn't say. Not for his son; he'd scarcely been any kinder to Josh than to her. And yet he'd refused to divorce her. He'd liked having a beautiful wife, the same way he'd liked having a luxury automobile. In a way, his affairs had been a relief, better than those cold couplings in the dark when, despising herself, she'd pretended to enjoy it in the hope it would be over more quickly.

She'd played the part of society matron, loved her son and endured her days trying not to remember that she'd once hoped for more. That for one golden afternoon she'd held everything in her hands. Still, she had her health and a wonderful son she loved, and maybe that was all she could expect. Maybe there were some mistakes that you paid for forever.

Or not quite forever because now Lloyd was gone,

killed, possibly by Roberto Mendoza, the man she'd thought for a few hours she'd loved.

The man who'd walked away without a backward glance.

Ridiculous to think it was impossible that he was behind the murder. She needed to believe it, needed, for Josh's sake, for it to be true. Lloyd had certainly had no shortage of enemies and Roberto Mendoza was maybe just one more.

She glanced up to see Gahan watching her. "Where do Josh and I stand?"

"Everything that you owned previously, you still own. For now, anyway."

She felt a little flutter of disquiet. "What do you mean, for now?"

"Well, it all comes down to what you can bring in." He made a dismissive gesture at the papers before him. "Your debt load is considerable."

"You mean Lloyd's debt load is—"

"*Your* debt load," he corrected pointedly. "You're responsible for all debts held by you as a couple and as I'm sure you know, you owe quite a lot."

But she hadn't known. She hadn't known at all. "What do you mean we owe quite a lot? There's the house and a few years left to pay on Lloyd's car, but that should be it. We own my car outright and we bought Josh's car used."

"I'm not talking about those kind of debts, although your second mortgage is certainly hurting you. It's the credit card debt that's the worst, the commercial properties that you've borrowed against."

"Second mortgage? Commercial properties?" Her

head was spinning. "But we paid off our credit card every month."

"Credit cards," he emphasized. "Several of them are maxed out, particularly the airline miles card."

"That wasn't our account, that was for Lloyd's business," she protested.

"He may have used it for business expenses, but it's a private card, Mrs. Fredericks. It was never transferred to Fredericks Financial. And you're responsible for it."

She resisted the urge to put her hands over her ears. Lloyd had never let her be involved in their personal finances, had become hostile and abusive any time she'd ever asked. Now, she understood why.

Consciously seeking calm, she let out a breath. "All right, how do I go about getting a draw from the trust fund to cover it?"

"Trust fund?" Gahan looked at her as though she'd just announced she was flying to the moon. "Your trust fund is gone."

"Gone?" She stared. "It can't be gone. It was twenty-five million dollars, for God's sakes. The income alone was more than a million dollars a year."

"I guess a million doesn't go as far as it used to," he said. "You spent down the capital about three years ago."

There was a roaring in her ears. "I didn't spend anything. I didn't...good Lord, it's gone? *All* of it?" Even she could hear the faint note of panic in her voice.

"The right investments—or the wrong ones—can eat up that kind of money pretty quick. Lloyd wasn't nearly as smart about finance as he liked to think he was. He wanted to be a player. Sometimes when you play, you win," Gahan said, "and sometimes you lose. Lloyd lost more than most."

"But he had money of his own."

Gahan studied her for a long moment, seeming to go through an internal debate. Finally, he let out a quiet breath. "The Fredericks family has been broke for years. Fredericks Financial has been struggling—the credit crunch hit it hard and it was significantly over-extended. You and Lloyd would have been broke, but he was good at arranging loans. He guaranteed the last one through your son."

Disbelief gave way to anger. "That's impossible. Josh only inherited his money a week ago. Lloyd would never have used Josh's trust fund to secure anything."

"Lloyd did," Gahan said simply. His intercom buzzed and he pressed a button on his console. "Give me five minutes, Colleen," he said, and turned back to Frannie. "Mrs. Fredericks, I'm sorry that all of this has come as such a shock, but there's really nothing I can do. My advice to you is that you talk to your family, arrange a loan. If they can secure your debts, you have as good a chance of moving forward as anyone." He rose and put out his hand. "I wish you luck."

Frannie left the office in a daze, scarcely feeling her feet as they slid along the carpet. It didn't feel real, nothing felt real.

Twenty-five million dollars, gone. Her father had left it to her when she was born, then died mere months later. She had no memory of him. But he'd loved her and wanted to provide for her, leaving the trust for her care, with the bulk to be awarded upon the birth of her first child. It was, she realized now, probably the real reason Lloyd had married her.

And now the money was gone, and so was Lloyd.

She touched her cheek, remembering the times he'd lashed out with his tongue. And, less frequently, his hands. He was gone and only she and Josh remained, trying to move forward through the morass he'd left behind. She pressed the elevator call button, the sound ringing in her ears.

"They grilled you for two days without pressing charges?" Jorge glanced over at Roberto as they walked through the police station parking lot to his car. "That's some lawyer you got. Or, excuse me, some lawyer I got you."

Roberto barely registered the joke. He glanced around, squinting at the sun and despising himself as he realized that he was looking for Frannie. "No charges— at least that's what they tell me right now. Of course, that could change."

"Why would they let you out if they were going to charge you?"

He shrugged. "Maybe they're waiting to get more information. Maybe they want to watch what I do."

"That could be a little paranoid, big brother." Jorge pulled out his keys.

"And it could be reality. It doesn't seem like they know much at this point."

"Well, they'll have to watch for a long time, because there's nothing to find unless you did it. Which I'm assuming you didn't."

Roberto opened the door and slid into Jorge's glossy

black Jaguar. "You ever think about putting your money into your business instead of pricey toys?"

"We're in different industries. In your line of work, a ride is just to get you to the lumberyard. In my part of the world, it's a branding statement." Jorge started the engine. "You didn't answer the question."

"I wasn't aware I was being asked one."

Jorge studied him a moment, then smiled faintly. He backed out of the parking slot and headed for the exit.

And for the first time in two days, Roberto felt like he could draw a real breath.

"You want to tell me again how you landed yourself in the hot seat? I mean, didn't you think we had enough trouble going already? You don't even know Frannie Fredericks." Jorge flicked a glance at Roberto. "Do you?"

There had been a time he'd thought he'd known her, but he'd found out he was wrong. He'd left her behind long ago—she wasn't why he'd returned to Red Rock. So why had he been idiot enough to go charging to the rescue? "I met her the summer I worked at the ranch."

And that quickly he was back to that day all those years ago, watching Fredericks stomp off and Frannie ride out like the wind, fury in every line of her body. When Roberto had caught up to her, he'd seen the tears. Somehow, comfort had turned to something more, to connection, to revelation. They'd lain down together in the soft grass under one of the spreading red oaks. And he'd shown her what making love was truly like, learned it for the first time himself.

"You knew her at the ranch? Is that why they held you? For chrissakes, Roberto, that was what, twenty years ago?"

"Close enough."

He stopped at a traffic light. "What makes them think that's remotely relevant? She wasn't even the one who got dead, he was."

"And he had pictures of me on his cell phone."

Jorge stared at him. "What the hell? Why would he do that?"

Roberto smiled faintly. "Maybe he thought I was cute."

"Even if there were pictures of you, anyone could have taken them. He could have taken them by accident. There's no way they can say that means anything. Any decent lawyer would shred that."

Jorge's lawyer had. But there'd been no explanation for the text message sent to Cindy Fortune: "Is this who I think it is?"

"What I want to know is what you thought you were doing by barging into the middle of this," Jorge said. "They're cops, they know their jobs. You should have left it up to them instead of trying to be some kind of hero—"

"What if she didn't do it, Jorge?" Roberto demanded. "What if it had been Sierra or Gloria or Christina sitting in that jail and I knew something that could get them off the hook? Would you still be pushing me to stay out of it?"

There was a beat of silence. "What happened between you and Frannie Fredericks?" Jorge asked quietly.

"Nothing," Roberto snapped.

Jorge drove in silence for a few minutes. "You know, even if a lot of nothing went on between you two, you don't need to take the fall for her."

Roberto turned to stare out the window. "I appreciate you helping line up the lawyer."

"You never have been any good at taking advice."

"You'd think you would have figured that out by now." Faint amusement replaced the irritation in Roberto's words.

Jorge grinned. "I'm what you call an optimist."

"How are Mama and Papa?" Roberto asked.

Jorge's grin faded. "Not good, especially when the cops showed up asking questions. I thought Pop was going to throw one of them through the window."

"Blond guy, brush cut?" Roberto asked.

Jorge nodded.

"McCaskill. Too bad he didn't, the guy could have used it. Hey, pull in at the bank, will you? I need some cash."

He was quick in the ATM. The enclosed space felt way too much like the cell he'd called home for the past two days. He just needed to be out; he needed to be moving. The hours of police interrogation had been bad enough; given Jorge's behavior, it didn't appear that the questions were likely to stop anytime soon.

Impatiently, Roberto pushed open the door that led out to the street. And came to an abrupt stop.

The recognition was instantaneous. It didn't matter that nearly two decades had passed since they'd stood in each other's presence. It was Frannie, he was as certain of that as he was of his own name.

She'd been striding down the sidewalk, not paying attention, but she was paying attention now, eyes wide, lips parted. They studied one another, taking a measure of what the years had wrought.

He tried not to let the shock show. "Frannie." It was her and yet not her. She'd changed so much, the vibrant young girl washed away. Once, she'd been laughing and mischievous, riding along beside him, playing jokes, teasing. Now, she was pale, cool and sophisticated to the point of almost not being there. There was a brittleness to her, a vulnerability hovering around her mouth that about broke his heart.

"Roberto." It was shock that had snatched the breath from her lungs, Frannie told herself, adrenaline that had her heart hammering. Surprise, nothing more, but still she kept staring, drinking in the sight of him, unable to look away.

And unable to keep from remembering that long-ago afternoon.

It was Roberto as she had known him and yet not: more lines, a wariness about the eyes. His dark hair was cropped short now, not long as it had been. Something about him had always made her think of a nineteenth-century bandit riding the border, tough and reckless. There was a strength, an uncompromising hardness in his face, yet in the Roberto she had known, that could soften into easy approachability when a smile curved his mouth, a mouth she knew was capable of passion and tenderness.

Frannie gave herself a mental shake. Hadn't she thought about this moment over and over again across the years, the dismissive glance, the cutting comment, the artful put-down? There had been a time she'd hated him. There had been a time he'd deserved it. Any sane person would think he deserved it now. Now, when he'd possibly murdered her husband. Now, when he'd possibly been the one to set her free. She straightened her shoulders. "I didn't know you were out."

"For now," he said briefly. "And you? They dropped the charges?"

"Not quite. They released me on my own recognizance."

"That's only because they don't want to admit they were wrong without another suspect. You've got nothing to worry about. You'll be all right."

"Of course. Everything's going to be fine." It was a lie. Everything was falling down around her ears, she could be back in jail any minute; someone, maybe the man before her, had murdered her husband. Yet she stood there in the sunshine as though she was just having an afternoon chat with an old acquaintance, mouthing platitudes, conditioned so well over the years not to feel that she'd maybe forgotten how.

And yet she couldn't stop herself from reacting to him, no matter how little sense it made. Maybe you never really forgot the first man who moved you.

Even if it had all been an illusion.

She swallowed. "Are you back to stay?"

"For now. The cops have me on the same leash as you. We're still trying to figure out who set the fires, I've got to finish some renovations on Red, and there are my parents to take care of, and Frannie—"

"What?"

He stared down at her. "I'm sorry about your husband."

How was it she wasn't?

Frannie shook her head like a dog shaking off water. "I have to go." She moved blindly past him toward where Josh had pulled up to the curb, his car idling as he waited for her, coming to pick her up after a visit to his girlfriend.

She got into the car, consciously not looking back.

Josh wasn't so subtle. He shot a glance over his shoulder at Roberto. "Who is that guy?"

"Someone I used to know a long, long time ago," she said.

And only then did she begin to tremble.

Chapter Three

The sun had long since set when Roberto stretched out on the couch, a Scotch at his elbow, a magazine propped up on his knees. He could hear the rush of the wind outside, the restless tapping of branches against the windows. He looked at the page, not registering the words, thinking only of Frannie. How many times over the years had he imagined her face? How many times had he thought he'd heard her voice?

He was grateful he was staying in the mother-in-law's addition to his parents' adobe, a separate space with its own entrance, affording him privacy where he could at last think about what had come to pass.

Funny how the two days he'd spent in police custody seemed like a flash, but the time he'd stood talking to Frannie—a minute? Two?—stretched out to become all-consuming. And yet he couldn't for the life of him figure out what he felt.

For a time after he'd left Red Rock all those years ago, he'd drifted, picking up work when he ran out of money. Picking up women, too. But time after time, night after night, he'd filled his hands with warm, willing female flesh, and found it wanting because it wasn't the right flesh, because it wasn't the right female.

Because it wasn't Frannie.

And he'd grown to hate her because he could never get away from the shadow of memory. All it would take was a whiff of scent, the sound of some stranger's laughter on the breeze to bring it all back. Because she was there, always there in the back of his mind, like a splinter that had worked its way so deep that the body could only form scar tissue around it. And part of him knew that no matter how much he might curse her inconstancy, her fickleness, her betrayal, that splinter of her would always remain somewhere inside him.

He'd settled, finally, in Denver, thrown himself into building a successful construction business. A man could make a million, then more when work was all he focused on. There had been women, of course, women whose laughter brought a smile to his eyes. But they never shared his house. And they never lasted, because eventually they ran into that scar tissue, that place inside him that could never be theirs.

He'd seen enough of the world since he'd left Red Rock to know that disappointment lay around every corner. He'd just learned it a little younger than most, and for that, perhaps, he should've thanked her. She'd helped him grow a skin of hardness and cynicism that had served him well over the ensuing years.

And he was full of crap, because all he could do was remember her face and feel an impotent fury at the thought of what might have been. But then what was he supposed to have expected from a young girl who'd grown up with wealth and privilege? A young girl who'd never been tested, a young girl who took the easy way because the easy way was all she'd ever known?

Except that was crap, too. He knew some of what she'd been through; he knew it hadn't been easy. So why, why had she thrown everything he'd given her of himself back in his face? Why had she cast aside everything they might have been together for a lifetime of unhappiness with an SOB like Lloyd Fredericks?

And why, after all of it, did he still want her?

In a burst of fury, he sat up and slapped the magazine down on the coffee table.

In time with the sound of the impact came a sharp rap on the outside door. Roberto frowned. Almost eleven o'clock. Jorge had taken to assuming he could come by whenever he liked, but this was taking it too far. Roberto wasn't in the mood for any more questions and it was time to tell Jorge so.

He crossed to the door and yanked it open. Only to see Frannie standing there.

"What the…"

She pushed past him, striding into the room without waiting for an invitation, a little gust swirling in after her. "What are you doing here?" she demanded, whirling on him. "Why did you come back?" Her eyes blazed blue, her hair flew around, full of static electricity from the wind. There was something of the witch in her then, something wild and uncontrolled. And her energy and agitation whipped up his own.

He closed the door. "You always just blast into people's homes?"

"You left. Why didn't you just stay gone?"

"What makes you think that's any of your business?" he countered.

"I don't need you here. I don't want you."

"And I don't want you. I came back because my family needed me here. It doesn't all revolve around you, you know."

"I learned a long time ago that nothing about you revolved around me," she retorted. "But what I don't understand is why you decided to get mixed up with Lloyd. All these fires, these cryptic notes floating around? Is that you?" she demanded, taking a step closer with each word until she was just inches away from him.

"Me?" He stared at her incredulously. "You think I'm behind all of this? Setting a fire at my parents' restaurant?"

"I don't know what you're capable of. I obviously never did. A man's been murdered and they had you in jail over it."

He turned away and reached for his glass of Scotch. "In case you've forgotten, *chica,* they had you in jail, too."

"You can't possibly think I killed him."

"You make a better suspect than I do."

"You know I didn't do it," Frannie snapped.

"I've been wrong about you before. But yes, I do." He took a swallow of the Scotch and set the glass down. "And just for the record, I didn't kill Lloyd, either. But I may have seen who did."

Was it his imagination or did she tense? "Is that why they arrested you?"

"They never put me under arrest. They were just asking questions because I came across what appears to be the murder weapon. Which is what got you out. You ought to be thanking me."

She raised her chin. "I didn't need you. They would have let me out eventually."

"They had you in jail for two weeks. When, exactly, were they going to let you loose? Especially when you wouldn't even deny it."

"I couldn't," she burst out.

"Why the hell not?"

She didn't answer him; instead she paced away, shaking her head.

"Why did all of this have to happen? Everything was going to be better, I had it all planned. Josh was going to go off to college, I was going to leave Lloyd. Everything was going to be okay, finally. But then it all started flying apart, and on top of everything else, you have to come back." Frannie rounded on him. "Why are you here?" she cried, pushing at his chest. "It was done, it was over. Why didn't you just stay gone?"

He caught her wrists. "You would've liked that, wouldn't you? After all, I don't have a multimillion-dollar trust fund or belong to the country club. You wanted me gone practically as soon as we got together."

"How can you say that? You lied to me. My God, one minute you were talking about how much you loved me and what you wanted for the future, and the next you broke and ran—without even telling me, without even a note. What happened, Roberto, did it get too real for you?"

Her voice rose. "Did you get scared when you realized you might have to stand behind all the pretty talk?"

"I ran?" He echoed incredulously. "What the hell are you talking about? I would have done anything for you. Anything," he repeated, his face a fraction of an inch from hers.

"Then why didn't you?"

"Because you sent your mother out to run me off." He'd been more naive than he'd had a right to be, thinking their feelings for each other would be enough. They'd ridden back to the ranch house that long ago evening, suffused with quiet happiness.

Or at least he had.

But they'd come back to a house lit up and a strange car in the courtyard, and the next night instead of Frannie coming to meet him as she'd promised, there had been Cindy.

Love, a life together. To Roberto, it had been simple but Cindy had made it simpler—clear out or get thrown in jail for statutory rape, with Frannie's testimony. He'd been a mistake. Frannie was done with him. The words had stirred only defiance—until he'd looked up from the dark barnyard to see Frannie staring down at them from an upstairs window.

"You sat up there and watched," he said furiously. "Don't act like you didn't know about it. I told her I wanted to marry you and she laughed and said you'd never marry me in a million years. You watched the whole thing."

And worst of all, she'd turned away.

Frannie's mouth fell open. "I watched the whole thing? Roberto, she gave me a note that said you weren't coming. I was inside with the lights on, I didn't see anything except my own reflection. And by the time I got out, you were gone."

"What was I supposed to do?" he demanded. "What was there for me here? Jail? I left because you gave me no reason to stay. And I stayed gone because...because I couldn't take seeing you again."

They stood, staring at each other as the enormity of their words sank in. The ticks of the clock on the mantle sounded very loud in the silence.

"That's it?" Frannie whispered. "It was all my *mother?* This is nuts, Roberto. This kind of thing happens in soap operas, not real life. Do you hear me?" Her voice rose, flirting with hysteria. "You're trying to tell me that it was all just a misunderstanding, that she played us for almost twenty years? Sweet Jesus." She dropped down onto the couch and buried her face in her hands.

Beside her, the cushions gave as Roberto sat next to her. "I don't know what's sane or insane at this point," he said softly. "I know what I was told, and I know what I did. And maybe we were too young, maybe it wouldn't have lasted, but I do know I meant everything I said to you that day, and I was ready to tell the whole world."

Frannie raised her face from her hands and turned to look at him. "Don't tell me that. I don't want to hear that." Because she couldn't bear to think of how different her life could have been.

Roberto reached out, his fingertips as gentle against her chin as a butterfly landing, and turned her to face him. "I never stopped thinking about you, Frannie. Never once. And I guess that makes me an idiot, because you married another guy and had a kid with him."

"We were so young," she whispered. "What we were feeling wasn't real. It would never have worked."

"Maybe, maybe not. Maybe this is all about another chance."

"How can we have another chance? Time changes people. I'm not the same person I was. Neither are you. That Frannie and Roberto are gone. What they felt is gone."

"You think so?" he murmured. "Let's find out."

And he leaned in to press his mouth to hers.

So many years had passed, each exacting its toll, changing the body, slowing the mind. How was it, then, that this was so familiar, so true? Nearly two decades had passed and she'd forgotten a million and one things in that time. But she remembered his kisses, oh, she remembered his kisses.

Even before his mouth settled on hers, her lips knew the touch of his—the softness, the warmth, the gentleness that he always brought. Lloyd might have said words of love in the beginning, but Roberto had made her feel them. With every touch, she felt cherished, wanted, enveloped in warmth. As though she were a sunflower turning toward the light, she felt herself blossoming.

How many times had he thought of this? How many times had he imagined the sweet scent of her, the soft coolness of her fingertips stroking his cheek? There had been other women, but always, inevitably, he'd found himself comparing them to his memories of Frannie.

And always, inevitably, he'd found them wanting.

He'd told himself that it was all his imagination, that no one woman could possibly feel so right. He'd told himself he was an idiot to even think it. He'd just gotten caught up in the same memory, month after month, year after year, and year after year it changed, like some internal game of telephone until memory transformed into a fantasy impossible for any reality to match.

That was what he'd told himself.

And in the moment his lips touched hers, he knew that he'd been wrong.

She was all that he remembered and more—soft and fragrant and sweet. They fit, purely and simply. Her mouth felt so utterly right against his, every touch, every move. Her hair spilled over his hand. And as he heard his pulse roaring in his ears, he understood afresh how the twenty-year-old boy he'd been could have returned from that afternoon under the red oaks utterly and completely thunderstruck with love for her.

He raised his head. Frannie stared up at him, her eyes huge and dark.

He slipped his arm around her. "I guess we've got our answer."

"No." She shook her head to clear away the haze. Her heart hammered in her ears. Life with Lloyd had been a battle for survival, but she had just about started to find the strength to start again. And now, to find herself so utterly taken with the barest brush of Roberto's lips over hers was terrifying. "No," she said again. "I don't think we've got any answer at all. Just more questions and complications."

"You're trembling." He held up her hand. "You call that a complication?"

"Yes." She shifted away from him. "Right now everything is crazy. I can't keep up. There's too much going on. The fires, the notes, Cindy's crash, Lloyd getting killed, I'm in jail, you're in jail, I'm broke, we're—"

"Wait a minute, back up. You're broke? I thought Lloyd was rich."

"So did I." She closed her eyes a moment and let out a long breath. "It's been a day for surprises. I met with my lawyer this morning and found out that my trust fund has been cleaned out, courtesy of Lloyd. I'm in debt up to my eyeballs."

"How did he manage that?"

She shrugged. "My fault, I guess. I was seventeen when we married, I didn't know much of anything about anything. I knew that I got the main bequest of my trust fund when I had my first child, but Lloyd managed our finances."

"And later?"

"He ran everything. If I ever asked him for details, even to see a stock statement or a tax return, he got furious. I gave up control without even a fight. And I guess once that happens, you can never really get it back."

"The best defense is a good offense. He didn't want you to know what he was up to."

"And it worked. I sat there in that office today listening to the lawyer talk about mortgages on office buildings and rental properties I didn't even know we owned."

"Don't beat yourself up. It's understandable."

"It's pathetic," she burst out, rising to pace. "I'm a grown woman and I barely even know my bank balance. He kept me in the dark, cleaned me out, and *I* let him do it."

"You're not to blame for it, he is. But he's gone now. Everything's going to be all right." Roberto came up behind her. "You and Josh will get through this, you'll see."

Frannie sighed. "Yes, I'll get through this. But I'm not taking money from Josh. His trust fund is for college, to get him started on life. I'm not going to siphon it off like Lloyd and my mother did to me." And she burned at the thought of asking anyone in the Fortune family for money. After a lifetime of watching Cindy beg, the idea of coming to them with her hand out made Frannie cringe. "I'll get through this," she said again. And maybe if she repeated it enough times, a miracle would happen and it would be true.

"*We'll* get through this." Roberto slipped his arms around her. "Whatever help you need, you've got it."

She turned to look at him. "I can't take your money."

"Sure you can."

"You don't understand. It's more than two million dollars."

To her surprise, he laughed. "Frannie, you don't know what I do for a living, do you? I own the second-biggest commercial construction and real-estate development company in Denver. I've got plenty of money, enough to help you take care of whatever problems you've got. More to the point, I can probably figure out how to make you a profit on those commercial properties that Lloyd's stuck you with. Don't worry. Leave it to me, I can fix it."

She moved away from him with a frown. "Haven't you been listening at all?"

"Enough to know we can take care of the details later."

"No."

"What?"

"No," she said again, her words stronger now.

"You mind telling me why, exactly, you're turning down help?" He kept his voice even, but she saw the little flare of temper in his eyes.

"Roberto, I appreciate the offer, I truly do. But I just found out that the man I've been married to for the past nineteen years took me for everything I was worth while I just sat idly by."

"I'm not going to con you."

"That's not the point. Or maybe it is. I haven't seen you for decades, I don't know you at all. And I don't know what we're doing here right now. We were kids when we were together before. Being in love at seventeen isn't real."

His eyes were hot and dark. "It felt pretty damned real to me."

"But that was at the time. I'm not that girl anymore and you're not that boy. For all we know, we could spend another hour together and start driving each other nuts."

"Judging by that kiss, I'd say that's a given."

"You know what I mean." She threw him an impatient look. "I just got out of a horror of a marriage. I can't turn around and dive into something else with you. With anyone. There's just too much going on."

"So that's it?"

"I don't know." Her voice rose in frustration. "I can't decide this right now. I'm not made of stone, I felt something here when we kissed, but what does that signify? Maybe what happened tonight just means that we got back that afternoon we spent together. Maybe it means a whole lot more, I can't say." She shook her head. "If anything's going to happen between us, we have to get to know each other all over again, don't you see? I can't just throw up my hands and turn the reins over to you.

First it was my mom controlling me, and then Lloyd.
I'm on my own now for the first time in my life and I'm
going to take care of myself. I've got to."

"I'm not Lloyd Fredericks."

"I know that, believe me, but it doesn't matter. I've
spent so much of my life reacting to him, following his
orders, living within his boundaries." She brushed back her
hair. She'd worn it long because Lloyd had preferred it that
way. "He didn't want me to go to college, so I didn't go.
He didn't want me to work, so now I'm thirty-six and I
don't have a clue how to make a living. For all these years
I've had nothing but Josh. There were days that I felt like
I wasn't even there at all and *I can't live like that anymore.*"
Her voice rose in a passionate torrent.

"I've got to figure out who I am. I've got to learn to
stand on my own two feet, and I can't do that if I'm leaning
on you. And if it means that working off Lloyd's debts
takes me the rest of my life, then that's what that means.
I have to do it myself. I can't let you take care of me."

"I didn't make the offer with strings attached."

"I know you didn't. But you have to understand, I
need to get past this on my own." She blinked. "Before
I can possibly be of any use to you or to myself, I have
to figure things out. I need to know what I'm capable
of. And I need to get Lloyd out of my head."

"I thought you didn't love him," Roberto said flatly.

Frannie gave a ragged laugh. "Are you kidding? I
spent most of our marriage hating him—when I wasn't
hating myself. And you. It's all a mess, Roberto. I'm a
mess. You deserve better."

"Let me decide that."

"I just…I need some time, can you understand that?

I just need time." She stepped in and pressed her lips to his cheek, then turned to the door.

Roberto followed. "You're going to leave, just like that?"

Frannie's eyes softened. "Not just like that. What happened here has changed everything. And even if there's nothing left once this is done, I'll always be grateful to you."

"It's not gratitude I'm looking for."

"Will you take friendship, instead?" She tipped her head. "Look at it as kind of a lease-to-buy program."

And as she'd hoped, he smiled.

"Whatever you need right now, you've got. And I'll take friendship." He caught her hand in his. "For now."

Chapter Four

"What the hell is going on here?" Hands on her hips, Cindy Fortune surveyed the confusion of boxes scattered around Frannie's living room and foyer.

Frannie went back to the box she'd been packing with books when Cindy had knocked on the front door. "Getting the place ready to sell."

"In this market? You'll lose your shirt, and this is way too sweet a house to give away. You and Josh could get lost in here. Hell, I could move in for a month and you'd never notice." A speculative look entered her eyes. "Maybe I will."

She kicked a box out of the way and sprawled on the couch, her brassy blond hair spilling over the back, long legs stretched over the coffee table. The ravages of time didn't stand a chance against the determination of Cindy Fortune, teased, Botoxed, lifted and liposuctioned to within an inch of her life. Seventy was the new forty, she was fond of saying, and she considered herself living proof.

As long as you didn't look too close into her eyes. Something hid there behind the false cheer—something that veered perilously between weariness and despair. But Cindy didn't like to think about that too often. Easier on the whole to toss down a drink or three and forget.

Frannie sealed her box and thumped down the tape dispenser. "Mother, what are you doing here?" Frannie had never even seen Cindy out of bed before ten, let alone ambulatory.

Cindy blinked. "Well, to congratulate you on getting out. I told those idiots at the police department that you couldn't have murdered Lloyd Fredericks, even if the pipsqueak did have it coming."

"I'm sure that was a lot of help." Cindy Fortune making a scene at the police station. No wonder they'd held Frannie so long.

"Anyway, I haven't seen you in a while so I wanted to stop by."

"That's right, you never did come to see me the whole time I was in jail, did you?" Frannie's voice was cool.

Cindy coughed. "Hey, well, you know me, kid. Jails aren't my style."

"Except for your DUIs," Frannie agreed, ignoring Cindy's sharp stare. Instead, she brought a group of framed photos over to the coffee table and set them on a stack of packing paper. Pushing her hair back behind her ears, she picked up the top picture to wrap it. It was Josh at his first Christmas, surrounded by gaily colored holiday paper and ribbons, laughing against her.

"I don't see why you have to put all that stuff away," Cindy groused, but Frannie noticed she didn't offer to help.

"Photographs are distracting. They make the buyers think of the current owners rather than imagining themselves happy in the home." She set the wrapped picture in the box and reached for the next. Times changed, she thought, glancing at the shot of her and Lloyd and a ten-year-old Josh on horses at a dude ranch in Montana. The smiles had all become a little strained, with a distinct hint of annoyance in Lloyd's eyes.

But it was on the next photo that Frannie's hands faltered. It was from a luau on a Hawaiian vacation taken just a few years before. Lloyd's eyes were focused off to the side—at the hula dancer he'd been flirting with, no doubt—Josh stood between them with a bored, sulky pout and Frannie…

Frannie looked lost, even in paradise.

How was it that she hadn't seen it before? Had she just lived with unhappiness for so long that she'd grown numb to it?

Her hands tightened on the frame.

"Anyway, if the place is too big, get another one," Cindy was going on. "No reason to unload this one."

"Yes, there is. I'm broke."

"Because you could just get another—*what?*"

"I'm broke, Mother, thanks to Lloyd. Remember Lloyd? The man I was supposed to marry because he'd take care of me? Instead of Roberto Mendoza?"

"Roberto who?"

The words came out a beat too late, a shade too innocent, and if she'd had any last doubt, Frannie knew now that it was all true. "How dare you," she said in a low voice.

"What?" Cindy asked weakly.

"I said how dare you." She stood. "Don't try to pretend you don't know what I'm talking about. I loved him and he wanted to marry me and you knew it." Her voice rose. "You ran him off like he was trash, and you made him think I was a part of it."

Cindy swallowed. "I…I did what was best for you."

"What was best? Look at this picture. Look at it," Frannie demanded. "Do I look happy to you? Do I look like I've had a good life?"

Cindy's gaze skated away. "That Mendoza boy would never have stood by you or been able to take care of you, especially when you were—"

"When I was what? Pregnant with another man's child?"

"Yes," Cindy whispered. "I did what I had to. You needed someone to provide for you. You were in trouble and Lloyd had a promising future."

"So promising he bankrupted me," Frannie said bitterly. "The Fredericks have been broke for years, apparently. I guess I was the last to know. Or you were. Lloyd blew through my trust fund and left me with more debt than you can imagine. So if you came here to hit me up for a loan or a place to stay, you're barking up the wrong tree." The words dripped with scorn. "The two of you were quite a pair. You bled off all the initial money when I was growing up and then he took care of the rest. And don't even think for a minute you'll get a penny from Josh. I'll make sure of it."

"Frannie—"

"Get out of here, Mother." She rounded on her. "I mean it. I can't even look at you right now."

"But…" Cindy protested. "Roberto Mendoza was just a man. He didn't matter. And it was so long ago. It would never have lasted."

"You made sure of that, didn't you?" Frannie's voice shook with anger. "Why leave it up to chance when you can lie? Especially when you'll never have to live with the consequences."

"It was for your own good," Cindy defended.

"For my own good?" Frannie repeated incredulously. "It was for your good, it always is." Whirling, she flung the Hawaiian picture into the fireplace, the glass shattering into shards.

Cindy jumped. "Frannie. I…I only…"

Abruptly, Frannie's fury was gone and in its place was only exhaustion. "Just go, Mother. Now." And she turned to the kitchen, leaving Cindy standing there.

Frannie had never been any good at fights. Part, she supposed, of why Lloyd had kept the upper hand. He'd relished them, going for blood every time. She'd always felt faintly sick from the roiling emotion, as though anger and hostility were toxic fumes that could overwhelm.

So she drifted from room to room after Cindy left, feeling shaky and unsettled, not finishing anything. Instead of continuing with the books and knickknacks, she found herself stopping at the long refectory table in the kitchen to pack up some of the dozens of albums of photographs she'd taken. But packing them turned into leafing through them, losing herself in the images the same way she lost herself behind the lens.

Next to riding her quarterhorse mare Daisy, photography had always been Frannie's truest escape. Lloyd might have done everything he could to block her from getting an education, but in this area alone, he hadn't managed to stop her. She'd joined a local darkroom co-op to perfect her processing skills, quietly taken what he'd ridiculed as hobby classes. She hadn't minded; she'd welcomed his derision—as long as he was making fun of her, he wasn't paying attention.

He'd never registered that she carried a camera with her nearly everywhere she went. He'd never heard about the handful of local exhibitions she'd been involved in. And he wouldn't have dreamed of escorting her to any event given by her friends, so he'd never discovered that she'd begun to photograph weddings and christenings. Outside of Josh, it was one of the few aspects of her life that brought her joy.

Too bad she couldn't make a living at it.

Or could she?

Eyes narrowed, Frannie began sifting through the images afresh, this time looking at them with an independent eye. She had a substantial body of work and a large amount of amateur experience. Could she turn that into a portfolio, put the word around to get work? Was it worth trying?

Could she afford not to?

A sound had her glancing over to see Josh walk into the kitchen. He was growing up, his once blond hair darkening, the face of the man he would become beginning to emerge. Somehow, when she hadn't been paying attention, the days had turned into months, the months into years and he'd become an adult. Just days before, she'd photographed his graduation. In another month or two, she'd be seeing him off to college.

Frannie swallowed against the sudden tightness in her throat. "Did you sleep all right?" He looked tired now, she realized as she asked, drawn somehow, thinner in his jeans and muscle shirt.

He shrugged. "Something woke me up. Anyway, it doesn't matter. Lyndsey and I are going to the lake today."

"Again?"

Ignoring her, he walked over to study the photos she'd laid out. "Hey, those are my graduation shots." Interested now, he sat. "Man, you caught it," he said, pointing to a shot of the class flinging their mortarboards into the air. "And I like this one of everybody lined up in their robes with no one's faces showing. It looks kind of like abstract art or something."

And then he fell silent.

Frannie didn't have to ask what picture he was looking at—she knew. It was a shot of him with his girlfriend, Lyndsey Pollack. Waiflike and blond, Lyndsey clutched Josh's hands in hers and gazed up into his face with that singular intensity that always made Frannie a little uneasy. Granted, teenage girls tended toward the dramatic, but Lyndsey seemed more prone to it than most. Never in all the time the two had been dating, as far as Frannie knew, had a day gone by without the girl calling Josh at least two or three times.

He pulled out his phone, and Frannie suppressed a sigh as she heard the simulated click of the device's camera, followed by the tap of his fingers on the keyboard.

"Isn't it a little early to start texting?"

She heard the bleat his phone made for an incoming

message, followed by more tapping. Then he glanced over. "Sorry, Mom, what did you say?"

She shook her head. "Never mind."

"Lyndsey's coming by in a few." He went over to the counter to pour himself some coffee, doctoring it liberally with cream and sugar. "She wants to know if you've got any more pictures of us at graduation. She's making a collage."

"I'll look." Frannie watched him walk back over to sit at the table. "You're going to the lake. This is the third time this week, isn't it?"

"Yeah."

"Don't you think you're spending a little too much time together? She's only seventeen. And you're going off to college next year."

"Maybe." He took a swallow of his coffee.

"Maybe what?"

"Maybe I'm going to college. Or maybe not. I've been thinking about sticking around here, instead. Take some classes at Red Rock Tech."

Frannie stared. "You're talking about giving up a full-ride scholarship to Texas A&M for a community college? And just when did you decide this?"

He flushed. "A couple of weeks ago."

"With Lyndsey."

"Yeah."

"It's not Lyndsey's decision."

A stubborn light entered his eyes. "Maybe it is. We're together."

"Josh…" Frannie bit back a sigh. "You're only eighteen."

"That's right," he shot back. "I am eighteen. That

means I'm an adult. You're still treating me like I'm some middle-schooler with a crush."

Frannie blinked at her usually easygoing son, the tension in his face, the sharpness in his voice. "Take it easy. I know you're an adult. But trust me, I was eighteen, too, and I can tell you for a fact that you don't know nearly as much right now as you think you do. Going to college will open up your whole life—change it in so many ways."

"Yeah, like taking me away from Lyndsey," he retorted. "That's what this is all about, isn't it? You and Dad have been trying to break us up since practically the day we got together. You don't take us seriously. You've never taken us seriously."

For the hundredth time, Frannie cursed Lloyd. They'd shared misgivings over Lyndsey's intensity, but true to form, Lloyd had tackled Josh head-on. And not surprisingly, the more he pressured Josh to give up Lyndsey, the more hell-bent Josh was on sticking with her. Frannie's instinct had been to gamble that Josh would eventually begin to chafe at Lyndsey's neediness. Now, though, with him threatening to give up his plans for a four-year college program—and she knew how quickly plans for community college could turn into dropping out—she had to say something.

"I'm not trying to break you and Lyndsey up, Josh. I'm just trying to get you to think about your future."

Josh's expression turned stormy. "This isn't about my future, it's about you not liking Lyndsey."

"I think Lyndsey is a lovely person," Frannie said carefully. But there was something about the girl that had made her uncomfortable from the beginning, an almost desperate drive to intertwine herself with Josh. Maybe Lyndsey was just an insecure high-school girl, but her expression in the photo had less a flavor of love than desperation. "Think about it, Josh. College Station is only a couple of hours away. If you go to A&M you can still be home on weekends and holidays and during the summer break. And who knows what happens after?"

He thumped down his coffee cup. "I've got a better idea. I start here and go to Red Rock Tech. Lyndsey and I can be together all the time and then we can go to Texas A&M later if we want to."

"But you'll lose your scholarship," Frannie protested.

"Who cares about the scholarship? I inherited my trust fund. I've got all the money I need."

All the money I need. "You're right," she responded. "You do have a lot of money now. And that means being more careful. You're going to have all sorts of people wanting a piece of you, coming to you with all kinds of deals to invest in. Or wanting to get involved."

He flushed an angry red. "Are you saying that Lyndsey's after me for my money? You're out of your mind. She didn't even know about it when we met."

"I'm just trying to get you to think about—"

"You're treating me like a little kid," he shouted, jolting to his feet. "Everything's changed, now. But you don't know what I'm dealing with, you don't know the spot I'm in and I've got to—"

The doorbell rang, interrupting the tirade. The silence rang.

Frannie's lips felt cold. "What have you done, Josh?" she whispered.

For a moment he stood, jaw working, and then he turned away. "I have to get this," he muttered. "Be there in a sec, Lyns," he called.

It couldn't be, Frannie thought numbly. He couldn't mean what it sounded like, he couldn't. She heard the snick of the dead bolt unfastening.

"Boy, you sure got here in a hurr—" Josh stopped. "Can I help you?" The words were flat and unfriendly.

"Is your mother here?"

Not the police again, Frannie prayed. She just didn't think she could take any more, not right now, not after all that had happened. She forced down the roil of emotions and headed toward the front door where Josh stood. It tugged her heart to see how protective he looked, holding it nearly closed, standing in the gap. He couldn't have done what she feared, not the boy she'd raised.

She stepped up behind him. "Who is it, Josh?"

And over his shoulder she saw Roberto Mendoza.

Nerves, pleasure and above all reassurance surged through her. It wasn't fair, not when she was still struggling to stand on her own feet. She couldn't afford to start leaning on someone. No matter how much she was tempted to.

Roberto wore jeans and boots and a snap-button denim shirt with the sleeves rolled up. With his black Stetson and his five o'clock shadow, he carried a flavor of, if not danger, then power and unpredictability, an ability to dominate any situation that came up.

No wonder Josh had gotten protective.

"You're the guy who was downtown yesterday," Josh asked, "weren't you? What do you want?"

"Josh," Frannie protested.

"You're not the only one who has to be careful," he shot back at her, then turned to Roberto. "In case you haven't heard, there's a lot going on around here right now. My mom and I are busy."

"Roberto, this is Josh, my son," Frannie said with a glare at Josh.

Roberto nodded. "He's right, you know. You do have to be careful." He stuck out his hand. "I'm Roberto Mendoza. My father runs Red and my uncle Ruben used to run the Double Crown. Your mom and I are old friends."

"Roberto Mendoza? The guy who—"

"Was helping out the police," Frannie interjected.

Josh gave him a swift, uneasy look. Behind them a horn sounded as Lyndsey drove up in her little red Toyota. "Josh," she called. "Come on."

Josh glanced between Roberto and Frannie, then grabbed his hat and backpack from the table by the door. "I've got to go."

"Josh, we have to finish this," Frannie began, but he was already bounding down the steps.

She let out a long breath and watched him get into the car.

Roberto studied her. "You okay?" he asked.

Frannie sighed. "I could use a cup of coffee. How about you?"

Chapter Five

Roberto knew he had no business coming over. She'd asked for space; by all rights, he should have given it to her. And he'd tried. He'd waited as many days as he could, but somehow that morning, he'd left the house to go to Red and instead found himself turning into her driveway.

"How did you find me?" Frannie asked as she stood back to let him in.

"Red Rock is a pretty small town. I made a good guess." Based on what he knew of Lloyd Fredericks, not Frannie. Certainly, the neighborhood wasn't the Frannie he remembered, this gated community of sprawling, pretentious, badly designed homes with security even a child could get around. In his case, he hadn't even needed a child. "A guy I went to high school with works the gate, so he let me in."

She was looking calmer, the high color fading from her cheeks.

"What's going on?" he asked.

She gestured at the packing mess. "I'm getting ready to put the house on the market. With luck, I'll make enough to pay down some of my debt."

"I wasn't talking about the boxes," he said quietly.

She shot him a hunted look. "Coffee first."

He trailed her into a kitchen that looked more like an operating theater with its glossy white cabinets and brushed-steel appliances. Hard, cold and soulless. Not Frannie, not even close. Then he glanced over the breakfront to see the photographs strewn over the kitchen table.

"Yours?"

At her nod, he walked over to get a closer look. There was a picture of a row of blooming cacti before a deep orange wall, a study in color and geometry and serenity. Underneath was a shot of groomsmen at a wedding. Instead of lining up stiffly, they'd gathered in a couple of pews of the church, some sprawling in the front row, some leaning over from behind, one standing. It felt like a moment captured in time rather than a staged picture. "Hey, some of these are pretty good."

"Gee, thanks." Her voice was dry as she reached into a cabinet to pull out a pair of mugs.

"No, I mean really good. You've got an eye for it."

She gave him a speculative look. "You think?"

"Yeah. Don't you?"

"Maybe," she said as she picked up the coffeepot. "I'm toying around with the idea of maybe trying to get a business going. You know, weddings, birthdays?"

"And graduations?" He held up the picture of Josh and Lyndsey.

She flushed. "I'm sorry you had to overhear that spat with Josh."

"I just caught the tail end. It happens. I remember having it out with my folks a few times at that age myself. Black," he added when she raised a mug with a questioning glance.

Frannie carried the coffee to the table. "Can you believe he's talking about giving up a full scholarship to Texas A&M for community college here so he can be close to his girlfriend?"

Based on what he'd felt for Frannie all those years ago, he could. "I guess you're not thrilled with the idea. Or with her."

Frannie sighed. "She wants to be with him every waking minute, share his every thought, even wear his clothes. Sometimes I feel like she just wants to, I don't know, absorb him."

"Sounds like high school to me."

"It's hard to explain. I just think they're too involved. They're still young. And don't look at me like that," she defended. "I'm fully aware of the irony. It's a different situation."

"But not to Josh."

"Of course not. It's part of what we were fighting about."

"Only part? You looked pretty upset when I got here."

She added sugar to her cup and stirred. "It's just all so crazy and it never stops coming. Every time I turn around it's something else. I was a widow, then a jailbird, then bankrupt and now I'm a single parent.

Who knows what's next? I couldn't hear your voice clearly at the door. All I heard was someone asking for me. My first thought was that it was the police."

"Not likely."

"How can you say for sure?" she challenged. "Lloyd's murderer is still out there. They're still looking for him. What if they haul me back in? What if they decide to arrest you? What if they decide to arrest—"

"Who?"

She closed up. "Anyone. It doesn't matter."

"*Chica,* if there's anybody on earth it matters more to right now than you and me, I'd be hard-pressed to name them." Roberto reached out for her hand. "You never came out and told them you were innocent, even though you are. Why?"

She pulled away. "How did you know that?"

"Not much stays secret in Red Rock for long. Tell me."

"I can't. What if I'm wrong?"

"What if you're right?"

"I can't be," she said passionately.

"Frannie." His gaze was unwavering. "For both of our sakes, I need to know what you know."

She shook her head mutely. Her eyes swam in despair.

"Tell me," he said softly.

"Josh." She swallowed. "I'm afraid it's Josh."

But you don't know what's happened, you don't know the spot I'm in—

"You think Josh had something to do with Lloyd's murder?"

"No," she said too quickly. "It's impossible. There's no way he could kill his own father. It's just that…"

"What?" He kept his voice gentle.

"He and Lloyd have been—were—at each other's throats the last couple of months. They fought at the Spring Fling."

"That doesn't necessarily mean anything."

"It was right before Lloyd was killed. Roberto, he could have been the last person to see him alive."

"Do the police know this?"

She turned to look back at him, eyes shimmering with tears. "How could I tell them? He's my son."

"Just because they fought doesn't mean anything happened. Did anybody else hear it?"

"A potter at the Spring Fling named Reynaldo Velasquez. And Lily. My brother Ross talked to her about it. He's a private investigator." Frannie dashed away the tears impatiently. "I was working the raffle tent for the Fortune Foundation. I went to the back to get more tickets and I heard them."

"What were they fighting about?" Roberto asked, getting to his feet.

"They were a ways away, but they sounded absolutely furious. Josh told Lloyd he'd be sorry, that he'd make him sorry, and there was something in his voice, something I've never heard before…hard, almost violent." She shivered.

He crossed to her. "What happened?"

She shook her head. "There was so much noise from the dance and the carnival and people walking by. And I got called away to help some customers. By the time I got done, I couldn't hear the fight anymore. When I went around to the back to look for them, I found—" Her mouth moved, but no words came out.

Roberto reached out and gathered her to him, stroking her hair.

"I dream about it almost every night," she whispered, her breath hitching. "I'm leaning over him and there's moonlight and I can see his blood. There's so much of it. I can't get away from it, I can't get it off. It's everywhere, all over my face, and my clothes…my hands… everywhere." And she wept then, giving in to the horror.

Roberto swung her up into his arms and carried her over to the couch, holding her, aching for her, hating the fact that he couldn't protect her from what she'd been through, that he couldn't wipe it all away. But he was here now and he'd do his damnedest to take care of her from now on.

The moments slid by and finally the cataclysm passed, leaving her wrung out and quiet against him. Finally, she stirred. "I'm sorry."

He stroked her hair lightly. "There's no reason to be."

"It's all just been such a nightmare. I've been numb. Until now." Frannie sighed. "I don't know what to do. How can I talk to the police about Josh?"

"The only thing that makes you suspicious is the fight?"

This time the sigh was longer. "That's not the worst of it. The night of the murder, the police found a pottery vase that had blood on it. They found it pushed under the flap of a tent." She swallowed. "I bought that vase. It was part of what made them suspect me. But I wasn't the last one who had it."

"Josh?"

She nodded. "He was supposed to take it to my car. Somehow, he never did. Instead, it wound up under the edge of the Fortune Foundation tent, at the back."

"But it's not the weapon."

She blinked. "It's not?"

"I don't think so. If it was, they wouldn't have been so curious about the bar that I found."

"The bar? What bar?"

"I saw someone leave the area where Lloyd was found, in a hurry, right around the time all the noise started. They tossed something away. Turned out to be a kind of a blue-gray crowbar thing, with stuff on it that looked a hell of a lot like…evidence."

She paled. "Oh my God."

"What?"

"That came from the Fortune Foundation tent. The table supports got jammed and we used it to pry them loose. The guys who were helping with setup dropped it at the back of the tent before they draped the tarps over." She stared at him, eyes filled with anguish. "Roberto, what if he really did it? What if he was trying to tell me today and he just couldn't say the words?"

"Do you honestly think Josh could kill anyone? Especially his father?"

"I don't know," she burst out. "I can't imagine it, but he was there at the right time. He could have swapped the vase for the bar. He made threats. And he's been acting so strange. He looks like he hasn't slept right in weeks and he's so on edge. He's never blown up at me like he did today, never."

"It just doesn't add up," Roberto said. "I can't see how the kid who was standing there protecting you killed Lloyd. Someone else did it, we just need to find out who."

"How are you going to do that?" she demanded. "My brother Ross still hasn't figured it out after almost three weeks on the case. What makes you think you can?"

"I have what you call a vested interest. Take me to see Ross and we can compare notes, set up a game plan."

"Roberto, you can't just take over here."

"And you can't be so dead-set on turning down help from anyone, especially me, that you put us all at risk," he shot back.

She opened her mouth then closed it. "All right, fine. I'll call Ross and see what he says."

"Good," Roberto said. "Keep me posted. Now where did we leave that coffee?"

They skirted the boxes and Roberto looked around the room. Lloyd Fredericks was dead and no one knew why. The killer was still at large, and maybe it was Josh, but maybe it wasn't. In which case, it wouldn't be a bad idea to stick close to Frannie, just to be sure she was safe.

"All right, that's one of your problems taken care of," he said aloud, following her back to the kitchen table. "Next is getting your house sold. It shouldn't stay on the market long. It's a nice-enough place."

"It's not a nice house, it's a horrible house," she countered, her spirit back, he was relieved to see. "Lloyd picked it out. It's so big it echoes, and the rooms are all at weird angles to each other, and it's in a Stepford neighborhood. It's true," she defended when one corner of his mouth curved up. "You look when you drive out. They're all alike. It's a good thing he didn't drive me to drink or else I'd have come home some night and pulled up at the wrong house and crawled into someone else's bed."

And before he could stop it, the image flashed in Roberto's mind of Frannie, silky and fragrant and wrapped around him. He suppressed it ruthlessly.

But not before he saw her eyes darken.

Roberto cleared his throat. "Well, you've got a guard. Some people like that."

"I wouldn't want to bet on our security team to take down anyone much more dangerous than a kindergartner." She picked up the mugs.

"At least you're safe from preschool gangs. Thanks," he added, taking his cup from her. "What kind of house would you have picked if you'd had the chance?"

"Something older, quirkier. Cozier," she added as she leaned a hip against the counter. "Wood and wallpaper, not marble and chrome. I'm going to look for something small. With Josh going off…to college, I won't need much space." There was a beat of silence. "But I've got to sell this one first before I can go looking. There's no way the bank would give me another mortgage at this point—I don't have quite Lloyd's gift for the con."

"You want me to take a look at those commercial properties you were talking about and give you my opinion?"

"Roberto," she said in exasperation. "How many times do we have to have this discussion? I can take care of my own business. I'm not going to turn around and let somebody else run the show again, including you. Especially you," she added.

The walls were back up, he realized with a pulse of frustration. All the years they'd lost, the life she'd had without him. If she'd at least been happy, it would have been easier to accept, but she hadn't and he hadn't been there to help. And now she was pushing him away, again.

But this time, he wasn't going anywhere.

"I told you, I do property development for a living. It wouldn't be free. I'd take a commission. I could assess what you've got, give you my advice on which ones to unload, which ones to keep, which ones to invest money in."

"No, okay? You can't come in here and fix everything. I'll get to it."

"Will you get to it in time?"

She raised her chin. "We'll find out, won't we? Right now, I've got to focus on two things—getting some kind of paid work, and selling this place. Assuming it'll move."

"It'll move." From ingrained habit, he'd been evaluating the house since he'd walked through the door, studying the ceilings and walls for clues to the bones underneath. Expensive, it might have been, but it wasn't well built by anyone's standards. With a little repair work, though, it would probably attract a buyer. "How long have you been here?"

"Five years. We moved in when they were first built."

He traced a crack in the plaster next to what he presumed was the pantry door. "You've had some settling. It happens a lot when developments are built on construction fill, especially if they don't compact it right."

Frannie followed him out to the foyer. "They must not have because we've got cracks all over. And half the doors won't stay closed—the latches don't catch."

"That's easy enough to fix." He nudged a loose floor tile. "You'll need to reset this. And once you get the cracks fixed, the whole place could probably do with a coat of paint."

She sighed. "I should start making a list. I'm going to need to get someone in to do an estimate."

"You know, I could do this work for you."

"Roberto—" she began.

Frustration rippled in his voice. "I rebuilt my parents' restaurant after the fire, but since then I've either been helping tend bar at Red or sitting on my hands, neither of which I'm good at. If you gave me this job—and I do mean job—I'd estimate it and give you a payment schedule. A payment schedule," he repeated firmly, when she would have interrupted. "There are a lot of clients I do that for. You'd be able to concentrate on getting your business going, and in return, you'd be doing me a favor. What do you say?"

She crossed her arms and looked at him.

"Look, I'm not trying to compromise your all-fired independence. This would be purely a business arrangement, customer and vendor."

There was a moment of silence.

"It'll sell faster." He gave her his best guileless look and was rewarded by a twitch at the corners of her mouth.

"Do you by any chance sell as part of your real-estate work?" she asked.

He raised his brows. "Sometimes. Why?"

"I bet you're good at it." And she put out her hand. "It's a deal."

"I still can't believe the police had the nerve to lock up Roberto just to grill him," Isabella complained. "I'd like to give those Red Rock detectives a swift kick somewhere painful."

"Tell that to Roberto," Jorge invited. "I'm sure he'd appreciate it."

They sat at a table in Red with Isabella's fiancé, J. R. Fortune, and Jorge's fiancée, Jane.

"I've barely ever spoken to Roberto," Isabella said. "What are we, third cousins twice removed?"

"Well, if you haven't much talked to him, that puts you in good company. He's not too chatty except with people he knows well," Jorge said.

"Unlike you." Jane reached for a chip.

"Is that your way of telling me I'm a silver-tongued devil?" He gave her a leer.

"Hey, enough of the tongue talk, you two." J.R. took a swallow of his beer.

"So, if Frannie didn't do it and Roberto didn't, then who did?" Jane asked.

"I don't think the police know," Jorge said. "They're still looking for information."

"I wonder…" Isabella stopped.

The others looked at her. "Yes?" Jane said.

"Well, I don't know." Isabella nibbled on her thumb-nail.

"Oh, come on, you can't stop there," J.R. complained.

"It probably means nothing, but remember when we had that fight?"

"You mean a couple days before you promised to fight exclusively with me for the rest your life?" he asked, his eyes glimmering.

She blushed. "That night. It was about a week and a half before Lloyd Fredericks got killed. I went out for a drink, like I told you, and there was a guy in there." The other three at the table all raised their brows.

"Now she tells me," J.R. said.

"Oh, it wasn't like that." She frowned impatiently. "I barely talked to him, although he was definitely looking to hook up. But the thing was, he had a fight with someone on his cell phone while I was there, and it sounded like...well, like he was being threatened." She hesitated. "I'm pretty sure the guy in the bar was Lloyd Fredericks."

It got their attention. "Did you tell the cops?" Jorge demanded.

"Not yet. I didn't know 'til now. I don't read the papers a lot or watch the news," she confessed. "I didn't see his picture until this whole thing came up about Roberto. The bar was pretty dark, and the guy didn't look just like the shots they showed of Lloyd Fredericks, but the more I think about it, the more I'm sure it was him."

"We need to get Roberto over here. He needs to know about this," Jorge said.

"I suppose. It's been almost a month, though. I'm not sure what I can tell him. The weird thing was, after he hung up, he looked all flushed and angry, but he said something about it being a telemarketer. That was what made it stick in my memory. You don't know the names of telemarketers, and he called this guy by name."

"What was it?"

She ran her hands through her hair. "I've been racking my brain trying to remember. It was kind of unusual, started with a *J.* Jonas, Jo Jo..."

"J.R.?" Jorge put in helpfully.

Jane swatted at him. "This is serious."

"See this, J.R.? Less than two months to the wedding and she's already beating me," Jorge said. "Don't say you weren't warned."

"You're so abused," Jane said, giving him a quick

kiss. "So, let's see, unusual *J* names. Um, Jasper? Julius? Jonah? Jocelyn?"

"Josh," Isabella said triumphantly. "That was it. He was talking to someone named Josh."

Chapter Six

The gray rock felt smooth and warm against Josh's fingers. With a hard snap of his arm, he sent it flying over the water to skip once, twice, thrice before it disappeared. A stone on water, out of its element and sinking.

The same way he felt.

"Hey, Josh, stop messing around and come sit with me."

He looked back over his shoulder to see Lyndsey sitting on the sand in her beach chair, his hat clapped on her head. He bent to search out another rock, adding a little more juice to get four flat, hard bounces before it went under. Out of its element, in an impossible situation.

There were lessons to be learned. Keep moving, first and foremost. If you kept moving, you wouldn't go under—if you kept moving and didn't let yourself touch anything for too long.

He wished he'd been smarter.

"Josh."

He sighed and turned back up the beach.

"Stealing my hat?" he asked.

She adjusted the brim. "I needed some shade. And black's my color. Anyway, who cares? You're more interested in rocks than me," she pouted. "Maybe I should be worried."

"Nah." He gave her a quick kiss and sat next to her on the sand. "I was just thinking."

"About what?"

He shrugged. "Stuff."

"Don't be such a worrywart. Things are going to be fine."

He studied her, her uncreased brow, her guileless blue eyes staring back at him—happy and untroubled. "How can you be so sure? What if my mom finds out that I—"

"That you're what? Going to be a dad?" She reached out for his hand and laid it over the still-slight curve of her belly. "She ought to be excited and proud of you. Everybody should. Anyone who's not, well, they can take a flying leap. We're not going to let anybody stop us, right? No way, no how."

A baby. As if everything else wasn't enough, there was this. "It might not be as easy as that, Lyns."

"Worry, worry, worry. You know what they say, if you worry you die, if you don't worry you die, so why worry?"

Josh gave her a tight smile. "Can we not talk about people dying, please?"

There was a flash of temper in her eyes. "Okay, let's talk about names. How do you feel about Cheyenne if it's a boy, and Piper if it's a girl?"

Josh leaned back on his hands and stared out over the lake. He remembered going to Six Flags on a class trip back when he was in fourth grade. All week, he and his friends had been daring each other to ride the great white knuckler. But it was so big when they had gotten there, so high, and maybe his mother had seen something in his face because she'd told him he couldn't go, he was too young. That had been all it took. Anger had made him heedless and he'd found himself fighting back until finally she'd relented.

And then he'd been in the train ratcheting its way up the hill and all of a sudden he'd realized what he'd done—acting without thinking, hotheaded—to wind up in the middle of something he'd never really wanted. But by then they had been at the top of the hill and it had been too late to do anything but ride it out. Sometimes that was all you could do. You made your choices, whether you meant to or not, and then you figured out a way to live with them.

Lyndsey, oblivious, was still talking about names. "What about Veronica? Or Cissy? That's the name of the nurse at the obstetric center. I think it's cute. Speaking of the center, I got my checkup and the doctor said everything's going just great with my pregnancy. There's absolutely nothing to worry about."

And with her smiling at him, how could he tell her that she was wrong, that there was everything to worry about? That when he thought about the future, what he saw were obstacles and chaos. To her, though, the path forward was crystal clear—they'd marry, move out, start a family and everything would be wonderful.

"I still think we should tell my mom," he said.

"And we will, when the time's right, but think about what she's been through, Josh. Why give her one more thing to worry about?" Lyndsey argued, twining her fingers around his. "If we hold off, it's not going to affect us. We're set for money now that you've inherited, so let a couple months go by. I'll look around for a nice place to buy, and you can tell her when we're ready to move out. She's not going to stand in our way now that your dad's gone. Anyway, you're eighteen, you're an adult."

He sure didn't feel like one, though. What he felt like was that little kid on the roller coaster, sick about what he'd done and scared stiff about what lay ahead.

"Thanks for driving," Frannie told Roberto as he helped her into the cab of his truck.

"No problem."

It was strange, she thought, as he circled around the front of the truck, but it felt for all the world like a date, with him coming to pick her up and opening the door for her and driving. Except that instead of going out to a movie or dinner, they were headed to San Antonio to compare notes with her brother Ross on a murder investigation.

Too much to think about. In the weeks that had passed since the Spring Fling, she'd discovered that the only way to stay sane was to simply not look at too much at any one time. Focus on the details, worry about what was directly ahead of her.

Except that what was directly ahead of her just then was Roberto.

"All set?" he asked as he opened the door and got in.

Focus on what was directly ahead of her, not the

look of his lean, long-fingered hands on the wheel, not on the jitters that ran through her stomach every time he got just a little too close. Because letting him get closer would be dangerous. If he could dominate her thoughts so effortlessly without even a touch, if she ever let him get truly in she'd be lost. She'd already had a taste of it that night at his apartment, that mindless, drugging wonder. Anything more could be fatal.

Roberto snapped on his seat belt. "You know where we're going, right?"

Straight toward the hazard signs, if she didn't watch out. "East," she said. "Straight to San Antonio."

Don't think, she reminded herself, instead focusing on the glossy blue hood of his truck. "So why did you drive all the way out from Denver? Why not fly?"

"I figured the truck would come in handy for hauling materials when I was working on Red." He started the engine. "Plus, I hate being crammed into airplanes."

"I can imagine." It wasn't just his height. He'd grown into a man since she'd known him before, with solid width of shoulder, heft of muscle. Even the cab of the truck seemed too small for him, though perhaps it was more force of personality than mere physical size that made her think so. There was a power to him, an assurance that he hadn't had at twenty. And underlying all of it, a smoldering sexuality that was fueled by confidence and intensity as much as by looks. She hadn't noticed it back when she'd been seventeen—maybe it hadn't existed yet—but it was there now, and as a woman, she found it impossible to ignore.

Focus on what was directly ahead.

"Anyway, the drive here from Denver isn't bad,"

Roberto was saying. "It took maybe seventeen hours, counting stops."

"You drove straight through?"

He coasted past the guard shack, raising a hand to his friend. "I like to get where I'm going."

"I'll say. I guess you're one of those goal-oriented types."

"I tend to stay pretty focused on what I want." He flicked a glance at her. "Don't say you weren't warned."

There was heat in those dark eyes, heat that ran through her and took her by surprise. She swallowed. "Seventeen hours is a long time to spend in a car on your own."

"I didn't mind," Roberto said. "It gave me time to think."

"About what?"

"Lots of things. Coming back, for one. What's going on with my family. Projects at work." He accelerated onto the highway. "Seeing you."

Less than a week had passed since they'd reconnected. It seemed more like a decade. Frannie turned to study his profile. "Would you ever have looked me up if we hadn't run into each other?"

"I doubt it. As far as I was concerned, things were still status quo. But Red Rock isn't that big and I figured that if I came back, there was a better-than-average chance I'd run into you."

From the time she'd heard he was in town, she'd simultaneously dreaded seeing him and wondered what it would be like. "Was it what you expected?"

"Not even close. I thought that after all this time, it just wouldn't matter anymore. But it did. You did. It felt like we'd just been out riding half an hour before."

"I know. It's so strange. It's been almost twenty years, but it feels like yesterday. I have to keep reminding myself that we don't know each other anymore."

"You know me."

"How can I?" Her throat tightened. "I don't even know what happened to you last month, let alone a decade ago."

"Ask," he invited. "You said it yourself, we have to get to know each other again."

Nerves skittered in her stomach. "I also said there was too much going on."

"Nothing's going on right now. We're just driving." He nodded at the passing hills. "Ask and I'll tell you whatever you want to know."

With so long a time, it was hard to even figure out where to start. "What do you do with yourself? How do you spend your time?"

"I've got a horse. I ride some."

"What kind?"

"A big bay quarterhorse. I call him Rocky."

"For the mountains?"

"For his attitude, mostly." His voice was amused. "He's a good match for me when I'm in a mood."

"I've got a little chestnut mare named Daisy that I keep out at the Double Crown," she said. "Too bad Rocky isn't here, we could race."

He was already shaking his head before she got the words out. "No way, I remember how you race."

"How long are you going to hold that against me?"

"How long you got?"

"Sore loser," she said, smiling. "So what do you do when you're not riding?"

"Mostly, I work."

"That's right, building your empire. Why construction? What made you go there?"

Roberto shrugged. "It was easy to find a job and I was good at it. Besides, I'm not all that crazy about being stuck inside all day."

He never had been, Frannie thought. There was something reassuring about the notion that a part of him she had once known hadn't changed.

"You must be good at it to have made such a success of yourself."

His teeth flashed. "I guess you'll find out, won't you?"

She'd taken him on without question to do the work on her house. For a person who was trying to take control of her own life, she hadn't done the best job with her first decision out of the gate. "I suppose if I were smart, I'd have gotten a couple more estimates for the work at my house," she mused aloud. "Compare prices and pick the middle one. Isn't that what you're supposed to do?"

"Depends. If you want it done right, forget price and pick the person who's going to do the best job."

"And are you the best?"

His grin widened. "Give me a couple of weeks and you'll see for yourself."

This time, the heat was definite. Frannie reached out for the air-conditioning vent.

"So that's it, Rocky and work?"

"Uh-huh."

"Nothing else? Nothing personal?"

His lips twitched. "What are you asking?"

Odd that she would find it so difficult. "Did you ever… Are you—"

"No," he cut in. "Never married, no kids."

She'd noticed the lack of rings, but it was a relief, even so. "Nothing?"

"I had girlfriends, but they were never permanent."

"I'm sorry."

"I wasn't," he said frankly. "It was always kind of a relief when things blew up and I found myself back on my own. I guess I'm like a junkyard dog, too territorial. Or maybe I'm just a self-absorbed son of a bitch."

"I doubt that that's true, otherwise you wouldn't be here. Anyway, it takes two people to make a relationship fail."

"Yeah? Is that how it went with you and Lloyd?"

With her and Lloyd, none of the usual rules applied. Except one. "We never should have gotten married in the first place. I knew it from the start. I never should've agreed."

"Why did you?"

"Because I—" The words caught in her throat. "Because I was pregnant."

He didn't reply right away, letting the silence be a balm. "I'm sorry," he said finally, his voice quiet.

Her chin went up. "I'm not. How could I be? Otherwise, I wouldn't have Josh."

"That's not what I'm talking about and you know it."

She shook her head, warding off his pity. "Things happen. I figured it out about a month after we left Red Rock. I told Cindy, just because I didn't know what else to do. She brought me back to confront Lloyd."

A moment passed. "And you're sure it was his?" The words were a little too careful.

"Oh, yes," Frannie said aridly. "He and his parents insisted on a DNA test after he accused me of sleeping around with everyone in town. But he knew it wasn't true and there wasn't much he could say once we got the results."

"It must have been hell for you."

She looked out the window, flashing back to that long ago chaotic fall. "I remember being twisted inside out, waiting to hear the answer. And even though I thought you'd run away, even though I hated you, I still kept thinking and hoping the baby would be yours. But it wasn't. And the next thing I knew I had Lloyd's ring on my finger."

She wrapped her arms around herself, cold now. "It's funny, I used to imagine sometimes that everything had turned out differently, that you and I were together, that Josh was ours. But then I'd remember how it ended between us." She swallowed. "It was like having a bruise that never healed. I'd get really good at not touching it, but every so often I'd forget and…"

The pain would be there, just as sharp as it had always been.

"It's history now." Roberto's voice was soft. "It doesn't matter. What matters is what we do from here on out."

But what she did from there on out could possibly be as perilous for her as anything that had come before. She didn't want to go from one man to another, dependent physically, emotionally, financially. It would be so easy to fall under Roberto's sway, like she had with Lloyd. And what would be left of her when it was over? She'd been through it once and she didn't think she could survive it again.

And so she turned to the window and watched the hills roll by.

* * *

"I'm not sure what to tell you," Ross Fortune said as he led Frannie and Roberto across his living room to the couch.

He was prickly, Roberto diagnosed—not happy about what he no doubt interpreted as somebody questioning his work. "Anything you can tell me is probably more than I know," he replied.

"It's not a territorial thing, Ross. There's a lot at stake. It would be good for us to know the details." Frannie's voice was firm, her expression soft.

Ross gave Roberto the kind of assessing look any brother would recognize. "Lloyd was a guy with plenty of enemies, I'm sorry to say, Frannie. How many of them disliked him enough to want him dead is another matter. So far, I've got no traction in working it out, and neither have the cops." He paused as they sat. "Can I get you something to drink? I can't offer you a whole lot— I haven't been spending a lot of time here lately."

"Anything," Frannie said.

Roberto watched Ross walk into the kitchen. The guy was rangy, solid enough to look like he could take care of himself if he had to mix it up. Darker hair than Roberto would have expected from Frannie's brother, and long enough to show he didn't give much of a hang about looks, which also netted him points in Roberto's book.

"I gotta say, you got my hopes up when they hauled you in, Roberto," Ross called over from the kitchen. "I figured that got Frannie and Josh off the hook. Too bad it was a washout."

"Sorry to disappoint you," Roberto said drily.

There was a hint of humor in Ross' voice. "Glad to

have you out, but I'd be even more glad if they'd find out who really did it."

Frannie looked out at the lights of the Riverwalk outside the window, her fingers twisted together in her lap. Roberto reached out and put his hand on hers.

"The problem is, I still can't put together a picture that means anything." Ross walked in with a glass of water for Frannie along with beers for Roberto and himself. "I've been asking questions, and nobody—" he stopped for a beat, eyes on their hands "—seems to know anything."

"Even the cops?" Roberto asked, amused when Ross handed him the beer from the side that made him take his hand from Frannie's to grasp it.

"Well, that's the question, isn't it? I've got a source in the department." He took a chair facing them.

"Right."

"I'm going to assume I can trust that whatever I tell you won't be passed along," Ross said, eyes on Roberto. When Roberto gave a fractional nod, he continued. "First of all, Frannie's vase wasn't the murder weapon at all. Right blood type, wrong DNA."

Roberto nodded. "I kind of figured that was the case. And the crowbar I found?"

"A match across the board—tissue, hair DNA," he said over the sharp intake of breath from Frannie. "It was the weapon that killed Lloyd. They pulled a couple of latent prints from it, a finger and a partial thumb, but they don't match anyone in the database. And they can't figure out where the damned thing came from."

"From the back of the Fortune Foundation booth," Frannie said, a look of strain about her mouth. "We used it when we put up the tent. I think they dropped it at the back before they draped the tarps over the frame."

Ross sat up. "The cops found the vase under the table at the very back of the booth, half-under the tarp. Somebody behind the tents could have shoved the vase out of the way and grabbed the bar as a better weapon."

Frannie's fingers clenched the couch cushions until her knuckles turned white. "Not Josh," she whispered. "Please."

"We don't even know if his fingerprints are on the bar," Ross reassured her. "All we really have is a fight between him and Lloyd and witnesses who could place him with the vase."

Roberto stirred. "There's something else you should know. About a week and a half before the murder, my cousin Isabella was talking to a guy in a bar." He exhaled. "She's pretty sure it was Lloyd."

Frannie turned to stare at him and he ached for her. "It was just a short conversation in a bar, Frannie, nothing more. But the thing is Lloyd got a call while she was there, a call that turned into a pretty nasty fight. She says Lloyd called the person he was talking to Josh."

Ross leaned forward to rest his elbows on his knees, fingertips together. "Hearsay. It wouldn't stand up in court. But cases are made of details and right now there are a lot of them adding up against Josh."

"He can't have done it, Ross." There was a note of entreaty in Frannie's voice.

"I don't want to think it, either, but we're starting to get a lot of information and sooner or later we've got to do something with it. Eventually, Lily and Roberto's cousin are going to have to talk to the cops. Eventually, you are."

"Ross, he's my son." Her voice shook.

"I know. That's why I've been holding off and I'll keep doing that. But I can't do it forever, Fran."

"Which means we've got to start finding some answers," Roberto said. Beside him, Frannie's breath sounded unsteady. "Hey," he said softly, "it's going to be okay."

"How can it be?"

He took her hands in his. "It will be. Trust me."

He held her gaze and suddenly everything fell away and it was just the two of them, bound together. The moment spun out and he let her fear dissipate through him, gave her back all the hope he had. "Trust me," he whispered again.

She blinked and shook her head, then rose. "I'll be right back."

If he'd ever seen courage, it was in the set of those fragile shoulders, Roberto thought, watching her walk away. He turned to see Ross Fortune studying him.

"You were at the Double Crown the summer before Frannie married Lloyd, weren't you?"

Roberto nodded. "For a while."

"And then you lit out and stayed gone."

"I had my reasons."

"Lloyd Fredericks made Frannie's life hell, and it hasn't gotten any better with him dead. She doesn't need any more trouble."

"I'm not planning on giving her any." Roberto kept his voice even.

"She also doesn't need a hit-and-run."

Irritation pricked at him. "You're making some pretty big assumptions based on zero data."

"I'm watching out for her."

"So am I."

"She's under duress right now. And vulnerable."

"Don't underestimate her," Roberto returned. "She's stronger than you think. And smart."

"Smart enough to know what she needs?"

"One of the things she needs, and I hope she's got," Roberto said tightly, "is a brother who believes in her." He let out a breath. "Look, I know where you're coming from. If it was one of my sisters, I'd be doing the same thing. So even though it's none of your business, I'll tell you that she matters to me, a lot. I'm here and I'm not going anywhere. Whatever she needs from me, she's got it. And if there's anything that I can do to take care of her, it's done."

Ross studied him. "She was the reason you came forward about the crowbar, wasn't she?"

"What do you think?"

"That you took a hell of a chance, as it turned out."

Roberto smiled faintly. "I didn't know they'd react quite that way."

"Would it have mattered?"

"No."

Ross was silent for a long time and finally nodded. "All right. Good to know where we stand." He picked up his beer.

Roberto clinked his bottle against Ross'. "Now that that's done, let's figure out what the hell I can do to help you find Lloyd's killer and get Frannie and Josh off the hook."

Chapter Seven

Roberto wedged the pry bar between the cover board and the stack of two-by-fours that formed the frame around Frannie's garage door. Between rain, sun and chipmunks, the wood was cracked, gnawed and peeling—damage that couldn't be covered by a coat of paint. Better to replace them altogether, he'd judged.

He set himself and pulled until the nails creaked. It was satisfying to feel the resistance, satisfying to do something with his muscles for a change. It gave him an outlet for the tension that seemed to run through him perpetually now, the ceaseless companion of his days and his nights. It was more than the unsolved murder and the arson at Red. It was the wanting, the need for Frannie.

Just being around her again was more than he'd ever hoped for and yet, with every day that went by, it was further and further from enough. Seeing her walk by, catching the elusive hint of her scent, hearing the laughter that came more and more often as the days passed only combined to make him want her more.

The hell of it was, he understood why she needed space. He couldn't imagine what she'd been through. Lloyd Fredericks, damn his soul, had very nearly extinguished hers. But he hadn't; the spark had survived and it was coming back.

And seeing it just sunk Roberto deeper than ever. She needed to figure out her life, though, and she wanted to do it alone. He'd agreed to give her the time to do it.

He just hoped he could keep to his word.

Dropping the bar, Roberto reached back to slide the claw hammer out of his tool belt.

He needed a bigger job, that was the thing, something he could lose himself in. A few hours and the current repairs would be done, leaving him once again to be sitting around jumping out of his skin. He needed a project that lasted for days, weeks, something that kept him working hard, hammering, sawing, lifting, carrying. He was built for effort and strain, not sitting around and getting soft.

Not for endless waiting.

He'd been working with Ross Fortune, asking questions, building up pictures, trying to find out anything he could about the fires at Red and the Double Crown, about the Spring Fling and Lloyd. And about a person in a hoodie that only he had seen. It wasn't enough to keep his mind off Frannie, though. None of it was enough.

Behind him, he heard a car pull up into the driveway. The rush of adrenaline had him shaking his head at himself. That was how pathetic he was. She'd been gone five minutes and he already missed her. Five minutes? Shoot, he'd begun to miss her before she'd even left.

Truly lame, he told himself, and yet all he could do was turn to see her with a ridiculous smile plastered over his face.

But the vehicle wasn't Frannie's tidy silver Volvo, and the person getting out of it wasn't Frannie, he saw.

Cindy Fortune slammed the door of the fire-engine-red Viper, adjusting the skirt of the white sleeveless sheath she wore. She took her time sauntering up, taking a long, slow survey of the work underway. And of him. "Well, about time she got this place fixed up a little. You get done here, I've got a few things you can do for me, sugar." She winked.

Then recognition hit. It was almost comical the way her expression cycled from seduction through shock, dismay and alarm before settling on livid. "You," she breathed.

And that quickly he was back in that dark barnyard, staring at her with impotent fury as she tore his dreams to shreds.

She looked now as though she'd be happier tearing him apart instead. "What the hell do you think you're doing here?" she demanded.

Roberto turned back to the door frame and set the hammer claw against a projecting nail. "Fixing the garage."

"That's not all you're fixing, I bet."

He ignored the comment. "If you're looking for Frannie, she's gone. It's her morning to work at the Fortune Foundation." With one swift move, he wrenched the nail out.

"Well, listen to that," Cindy said nastily. "He even

knows her schedule. You didn't waste a minute moving in on her, did you? I guess you think you're pretty cute."

"I'm not moving in on anything." In quick sequence, he ripped out the other nails and tossed the loose board aside on the grass nearby. "I'm just helping her get the house ready to sell."

"Oh, sure, helping out the poor little widow."

"Someone should be a help to her." He set the crowbar to pry off the next two-by-four in the stack.

"She doesn't need your kind of help."

He turned to her. "With you around? I think she can use all the help she can get."

"What do you think you're going to do, cozy up to her and take her for all she's got?"

"I think you and Lloyd already took care of that."

"Oh, you've got an angle." The words dripped with scorn. "Your type always does."

"You don't know what my type is. You never bothered to find out." He dropped the crowbar. "You were too busy sticking your daughter with that miserable excuse for a human being."

"Lloyd Fredericks was worth ten of you."

"Doesn't look that way now, does it? But I guess at the time, you were hoping the two of you would become good friends. Maybe good enough that he texted you just before he was killed." Roberto strode into the garage to his toolbox.

She followed him. "What are you talking about?"

"He sent you my picture from the Spring Fling. What else did he send? Who was he meeting there?" He rounded on her. "Help your daughter."

"I don't know what you're talking about."

"And maybe you know a whole lot more than you're saying."

Her eyes narrowed. "Don't you point the finger at me. You're the one they had in jail."

"But Frannie's the one they filed charges against and they haven't dropped them. It could be her freedom at stake. For once in your life, look past your own nose and do something to help her."

"I always took care of her," she said hotly.

"Who are you trying to kid?" His voice was incredulous. "Do you have any idea what her life was like with that creep?"

"I did what was best for her."

"You did what was best for *you*," he shot back. "I'm not sure what you got out of it—maybe Lloyd threw a few checks your way—but don't ever think you can fool anyone into thinking you did any of it for Frannie's benefit."

"I suppose that's what you're telling her. You're trying to turn her against me, aren't you? Well, it won't work," Cindy snarled. "I know all about trash like you. I ran you off once before and I'll run you off again."

"Try it," he invited. "Go ahead, take me on. We're not kids anymore and I'm more than a match for you. Give it up, Cindy."

"Don't you tell me what to do, you parasite," she shouted, pure fury distorting her features.

A clank behind them had them both spinning. Josh stood at the edge of the garage where sunlight met shadow. "Hey," he said weakly.

Alarm flashed over Cindy's face. "Josh, my God, where did you come from? You scared the life out of me."

"Lyndsey dropped me off. What's going on?"

"Oh, nothing," she said, her gaze jumping nervously between Roberto and Josh. "Isn't that right, Mr. Mendoza?"

Roberto wasn't particularly crazy about jumping in on Cindy's side, but there was no sense in dragging the kid into her histrionics. That said, Josh had grown up with Cindy as his grandmother. He probably had a pretty good idea what she was like. He certainly didn't look convinced by her attempts to gloss things over.

Roberto cleared his throat. "I need to get back to work," he said, fishing a chisel out of his toolbox.

"Give me a hug, baby." Cindy crossed over to kiss Josh. "I didn't know you were around."

"I couldn't miss my best boy's graduation, could I?"

Josh gave her a cynical look. "That was a week ago."

"Oh…of course," she floundered. "I, uh, meant I couldn't miss celebrating it with you. Sorry I wasn't at the ceremony. Something came up."

"It usually does," Josh said.

"I'll make it up to you. We'll go out to the mall, buy you something."

Josh shook his head. "Don't worry about it, there's nothing I need." He turned to watch Roberto.

Cindy just stood a moment, ill at ease, glancing between the two of them. She was clearly dying to ask when Frannie would be back, Roberto realized in sour amusement, but she wasn't about to give him the satisfaction. Finally, she turned toward her car.

"Well, I can't stay around all afternoon. Tell your mom…" She hesitated. "Tell her I stopped by," she said to Josh.

"Okay." He watched her get into her car and drive away.

Roberto, meanwhile, was stripping out the rest of the nails from the last board. He felt, more than saw, Josh staring at him.

"What were y'all fighting about?"

Roberto pulled the board loose and tossed it onto the grass near the other. "I'd say that's between us."

"It sounded like it had something to do with my mom. That makes it my business."

"No, that makes it your mom's business."

"Yeah? You going to tell her about it?"

"Not if I don't have to. She doesn't need any more grief right now." Roberto picked up one of the replacement boards and got out his tape measure to check the length.

Josh let his backpack drop to the ground. "So, what's the deal with you and my mom?"

"That's also your mom's business."

"She's not here. I'm asking you." He raised his chin. "I've never seen you before, my dad gets killed, and all of a sudden you're showing up around the place. You got something going on with her?" There was an edge to the kid's voice made up as much of anxiety as challenge.

He'd stood at the door to protect his mother, Roberto remembered. And maybe he deserved a little straight talk.

He leaned the board up against the door frame. "You mean are we having an affair? No. Until last week, I hadn't seen your mother for almost twenty years."

The cynical look returned. "And now you just happen to be here. You expect me to buy that?"

"I don't expect you to buy anything," Roberto said evenly. "You asked, I answered. I happened to be here to see family and your mother and I ran into each other."

"They arrested you for my father's murder, didn't they?" Something flickered in Josh's expression, something that Roberto couldn't quite identify.

"No, they just asked me some questions."

"Then why'd they lock you up?"

"They thought I knew some things that I didn't."

"What?" Josh's gaze skated away, over to the crowbar lying on the driveway.

Roberto watched him. "Legally, I can't tell you. All you need to know is that it got your mom out."

"Is that why you went to the cops, so they'd let her go? Whatever happened with you guys must have been a big deal for you to do that after all this time."

"We were…friends, for a little while."

"More than friends."

"Definitely not your business."

"Definitely more than friends," Josh said, nodding to himself. "But I guess it didn't last. I heard what my grandmother said about running you off. Is that what she did? You and my mom hooked up twenty years ago and she didn't like it? She wrecked things?"

There was an intensity in the kid's eyes that went far beyond curiosity. "There's more to it than that, but yeah, basically."

Josh glared upward, shaking his head. "I don't freakin' believe it," he exploded, spinning to slam his palm against the garage-door frame.

"Hey," Roberto said.

"Man, parents are so full of it. For the whole last year, almost since Lyndsey and I got together, all my mom and dad could do was try to break us up. And now you tell me that she went through the same thing with you?" He cursed. "You'd think she would've remembered what it was like and gotten my dad off my back. I mean, he was always on me, you know? It was like I was eight instead of almost eighteen, and he's ordering me around and yelling and talking all this trash about Lyndsey, I mean trash, and telling me what I can and can't do and getting in my face until I swear I just wanted to knock his damned head—" He stopped abruptly.

"Yeah?" Roberto stayed absolutely still.

Josh looked down, reddening. "I'm just saying that. I didn't mean for real."

"Sure." Roberto studied him, the high color, the agitation, the fear that came off him in waves. "But it doesn't matter how your dad acted now, does it? He can't stand in your way anymore."

"He sucked," Josh muttered. "I hated the way he treated my mom. I hated him. But I didn't want him dead."

"No?"

"No."

"Who did?"

"I don't know." Josh shifted his feet and looked away.

"They could still take your mom in at any time. You want that to happen?"

"No! I never wanted that. That was the worst."

"Well, she's out for now and I want to keep it that way. If you know anything about the murder, you'd better tell me."

"I don't," Josh said, staring at the crowbar. "I don't know anything at all."

"Well?" Lily looked expectantly at Frannie. "How did it go?"

The café was a little slice of Europe on Red Rock's

Main Street, with snowy-white linen, wrought-iron chairs and baskets of crimson geraniums hanging from the glossy green lampposts along the curb. It was unseasonably cool for June, which in Texas meant it was just right for lunch outdoors.

Frannie sat down, propping her portfolio case against the chair. "How did it go? I was a nervous wreck. My hands are still shaking," she confessed, holding them up. "See?"

"How can you be nervous? Nick Fortune is your cousin. You see him every week at the Fortune Foundation when you volunteer. And Emmett and Linda. They don't bite."

"But they do run the Foundation. It's one thing to see them when I'm helping out. It's another to be looking at them across a conference table, trying to convince them to hire me." The breeze pushed a lock of hair into her face and Frannie tucked it behind her ear impatiently.

"I don't see what the problem is," Lily said, signaling to the waiter inside the café. "You have something to offer, a service that they need."

"I'm sure they have their choice of fancy marketing agencies to do the photographs for the new Foundation brochure. They don't need me."

But it was worth taking a chance to see if they might. If nothing else, it was good practice. All things considered, the meeting had gone better than Frannie had expected. She hadn't detected any signs of surprise when they looked at the portfolio, which gave her confidence that she hadn't done anything wildly wrong. For the pitch, she'd gone with her instincts. Now, she just had to wait for their decision.

"So, what did they say?"

"They're still interviewing photographers. They

expect to decide next week." It was a long shot, but if she came through it would be a big win—her first professional job, one that would lead to others.

She hoped.

"Why the big rush to start a business?" Lily asked as the waiter filled Frannie's water glass. "I mean, I can understand that you'd want something to do now that Lloyd's gone, but with everything that's going on right now, wouldn't it be better to wait?"

"I can't wait." The words were too quick, the desperation in her voice a little too naked. "I mean, I want to get it going," she said more moderately. "You know, take my mind off things."

"I can appreciate that, but isn't there a better way? One that doesn't give you more stress to deal with?"

"I need to do this, Lily." She kept her voice low, for the pedestrians walking beside their table.

"Why?" Lily stared at her. "What's going on, Frannie?"

She let out a breath. "This is for you and you alone to know, all right?"

Lily nodded.

"Lloyd left me with a lot of debt, Lily, a lot. And he never bothered to get life insurance."

"He always seemed like one of those guys who figured he'd live forever."

"Yeah, but he was wrong. He left me in a deep hole and I've got to figure out a way to get out of it."

Lily turned for her purse. "Well, that's easy," she said briskly. "How much do you need?"

"None, Lily. I don't want your money. I need to do this myself."

"Fine, we'll make it a loan."

"Put the checkbook away," Frannie told her. "Please. I'm not Cindy, I can't come to you with my hand out."

Lily's eyes softened. "Sweetheart, you could never be like Cindy in a million years. And money isn't an issue. We've got scads of it, we can get you whatever you need."

"What I need, for once in my life, is to take care of myself." Frannie looked at her, eyes pleading. "Everybody wants to help—you, Ross, William, Roberto—but I need to do this alone. I've been depending on other people for way too long."

"Roberto? Roberto Mendoza? What's he got to do with all of this?" Lily frowned. "Frannie, the police were questioning him about the murder. You shouldn't even be talking to him. It'll just make things worse."

Frannie smoothed her hair back. "I'm still charged with Lloyd's murder, Lily. They could haul me back in at any time. How can it possibly be any worse?"

"How dare you show your face here?" a voice hissed venomously.

Frannie jolted and glanced up to see a cadaverously thin blond woman stopped on the sidewalk, staring at them. Lloyd's mother, Jillian Fredericks. Frannie had been wrong. Things could get worse.

A whole lot worse.

Chapter Eight

"How did you get them to let you out?" Jillian's voice was low and hostile.

Frannie raised her chin. "They finally realized they didn't have enough evidence to hold me."

"Oh, I'm sure. After all, you're related to Ryan Fortune," she sneered. "Nothing that goes on with you people in this town should surprise me. But we all know how you really got out."

"The way I got out was by having nothing to do with Lloyd's murder."

"You're lying. You have been from the beginning. You trapped him into marrying you."

"*I* trapped *him?*" Anger began a slow burn in her. "You have no idea what you're talking about, Jillian. If anyone set a trap, it was Lloyd."

"I doubt that very much."

Frannie's gaze was very direct. "Do you?"

She remembered that night, the one that had changed her life forever. A party thrown by some of Lloyd's fraternity brothers. He'd shown her off, introduced her to Long Island iced teas and taken her, stumbling, to a back room. He'd been insistent and she'd been in no condition to protest. *It'll be good,* he'd said, *I promise.* But it hadn't been. He'd been too rough, too eager, too focused on his own pleasure to have a care for hers as he'd stripped her of her innocence.

She'd sworn she would never allow Lloyd to touch her again. But when she'd told him the next day, he'd railed at her, accusing her of sleeping with Roberto. "You think you can throw me aside for some hired hand?" he'd demanded. "I'll make you sorry."

She'd fled on horseback, but Roberto had followed. And heartache had come on their heels.

I'll make you sorry, Lloyd had promised.

And he'd spent nineteen years doing just that.

"You're lying." Jillian's eyes glittered. "You've always lied."

"You know it's the truth."

"Don't you talk about my Lloyd." Her voice rose. "You held him back. You were never good enough for him, ever. He could have married anyone and he settled for you, you little round-heeled piece of trash. You're nothing, Frannie Fortune, nothing," she spat. "I hope they send you to jail to rot."

Lily shot to her feet. "That's enough, Jillian."

Jillian turned her malevolent gaze to Lily. "That's enough, all right, enough of you Fortunes."

Frannie raised her hand. "Lily, let me handle this.

Jillian, I'm sorry about Lloyd," she said evenly. "No mother should lose her child, and maybe that kind of pain can make a person say anything. But you're out of line and this is no place for a scene."

Jillian shook off the friends who were trying to draw her away. "You want a scene? Just wait. Everyone knows you killed him. There's blood on your hands. I don't care who you bribed to let you out, everyone knows you did it. And I'll make sure you pay for it."

And she turned away, leaving Frannie shaking.

"Are you all right?" Lily asked.

Frannie took a deep breath and let it out. "I should be. You'd think I'd be used to her after all this time."

Lily frowned. "I don't like to be unkind about anyone, but I really think Jillian is not right in the head. I think the strain of Lloyd's murder has sent her off. I hope Cordell gets her some help."

"She's always been that way, Lily. You can't imagine how awful she was to live with." Frannie remembered the weekly visits, the phone calls, the steady drip of poison in Lloyd's ear every time he talked to his mother. "Nothing was ever good enough for her, nothing I said, nothing I did. Anything nice I ever tried to do she threw back in my face. If it wasn't Lloyd ordering me around, it was Jillian, always trying to butt in with Josh and Lloyd, telling me how to decorate the house, what to do, what to wear, how to move, how to think, how to breathe." She took a deep breath. "I was a doormat, but I'm done with that now, it's over."

And it was as she said the words that she realized it really was. Lloyd's hatefulness, Jillian's hostility weren't a part of her life anymore. She didn't have to swallow her frustrations, put aside her desires, turn the other cheek to keep the peace, accept an unacceptable situation. She could live her life without compromise.

She turned to Lily with shining eyes. "Things are going to change."

Lily raised her water glass for a toast. "To your new life. To no more Jillian."

They clinked glasses. "No more sitting home all day waiting for something bad to happen," Frannie marveled.

"No more Stepford house."

"No more parties with people I hate."

Lily toasted her again. "No more mean people," she said.

"No more spending three days cooking Thanksgiving dinner, only to spend eight hours listening to Jillian tear it apart," Frannie countered.

"Oh, double toast on that one," Lily said.

Frannie's laughter turned into a sputter as the breeze blew a lock of hair into her open mouth. "Gack," she said, pulling out the strands. "No more eating my own hair. No more—" She broke off, staring across the street.

Lily raised a brow. "No more…whatever it is you're staring at?"

Frannie turned to her, mouth curving. "Would you mind if I skip out on lunch?"

"Skip out on lunch? Not a chance. Wherever you're going with that look in your eye, I'm going with you." Lily threw a bill on the table and rose to follow Frannie. "And just where are we going, anyway?"

Frannie laughed. "To do something I should have done a long time ago."

* * *

The glossy blue bulk of Roberto's truck blocked Frannie's driveway, forcing her to stop partway up the concrete apron. She got out to the sharp reports of hammer blows. Roberto was at work on the garage, she saw, craning her neck to glimpse the top of his head over the truck. She headed toward the front of the truck to find him.

And stopped in her tracks.

Roberto wore jeans and a plain T-shirt, his tanned skin dark against the white cotton. A leather tool belt was slung about his hips, making them look very narrow. A nail dangled from his lips like a cigarette. As she watched, he picked it out and positioned it against the board with one hand. With the other, he brought the hammer around in a sweeping arc and with a single blow drove the nail all the way into the wood.

Her lips parted.

He shifted and slammed in nail after nail, smoothly, rhythmically and with deceptive speed. There was an assurance, an insouciant grace in his every motion. Muscle flexed in his back, rippled in his forearms. She'd never seen a man who inhabited his body so completely. It made her think of some lithe, powerful animal like a jungle cat. She stared, transfixed.

He'd finished and was turning to pick up his tools when he saw her.

Time went by—seconds? Minutes?—she couldn't say because for just that time they didn't speak, didn't move, only locked eyes with each other. And then he was walking toward her, slipping his hammer into the tool belt without a glance. His eyes looked black, even in the sun. Her lungs snatched a breath of their own accord.

"You cut your hair."

She swallowed. "It was getting in my way."

"I like it."

There was something in his voice, some vibration that set up an answering thrum deep within her.

Straight toward the hazard signs.

You shouldn't even be talking to him.

The breeze caught up the strands of her hair and tossed them around. In his eyes, there was desire, but also something far more seductive—delight. "I remember the first time I saw you," he said softly, reaching out to brush her bangs off her forehead. "You'd just gotten out of the car. You were wearing this little white skirt and a pale green shirt with no sleeves. You reminded me of one of those pixies in the Disney movies."

It took her a moment to find her voice. "I didn't think you noticed me."

"I noticed you. Maybe you wouldn't say boo to a goose when you got there, but even then you had this look like you were fixing to make some kind of trouble."

"What trouble did I ever cause?"

"Besides distracting me every minute of every day?"

"You can't blame me for that," she said, moistening her lips.

"What about the fact that I haven't gotten a decent night's sleep since I hit town?"

He was too close, she thought, close enough that she could feel the heat radiating off of him.

"Show me what you're working on," she said with effort.

He studied her. "I think you know what I'm working on."

The seconds stretched out. She could feel each individual thud of her heart.

His teeth gleamed and he turned. "But if you want to see what you're paying for, I just finished putting in the new frames around the garage doors. It's supposed to rain tonight and tomorrow, so I'll have to wait to paint them until the weather cooperates."

"Nice job," she said, but she wasn't focusing on the wood. She was remembering the first time she'd ever seen him. He'd been lankier then, his hair longer, flowing thick down to his collar. He'd seemed so serious that she'd been afraid to talk to him. But she'd discovered that what she'd taken for brooding had been simple thoughtfulness, that he was also capable of laughter. He'd been genuinely interested in what she had to say instead of talking over her the way Lloyd had. Lloyd's idea of wooing her had been concerts and rides in his sports car. He'd never understood that the truest seduction was simply listening.

But then, he'd never understood her, period.

Roberto walked into the garage and picked up his toolbox. "I'm done out here. Why don't you show me those doors that don't latch and I can get to work on them?"

The interior of the house was cool and dim after the bright sunlight of the outdoors. "Do you want something to drink?" Frannie asked as they walked into the kitchen.

Roberto set down the toolbox. "Water would be great."

She reached into a cupboard and pulled out a glass, conscious of the way his eyes followed her as she went to the refrigerator to fill it. Such a simple thing, and yet there was something oddly intimate about the act of setting it down before him and watching him drink, his throat moving as he swallowed.

"Thanks," he said when he'd finished, handing her the glass. For a fraction of a second, their fingers brushed and she felt the heat bloom up her arm. "All right, where are those doors?"

Frannie set down the glass by the sink. "The pantry door right here, the door to the hall bathroom, the den, the—"

"Hold on. That's enough for starters. When you said half the doors in the house didn't close, I thought you were joking."

"Trust me, there are more."

"I'll let you know when I'm ready for them." He set down his toolbox by the pantry door and set to work.

She'd been wary of having him work on the house because she'd feared him getting too involved in her life. She hadn't considered the hazard of simply having him around for hours at a time, watching him make repairs with those clever, capable hands.

And being unable to forget what they'd felt like on her skin.

So she tried to distract herself by going back to packing. It didn't help, though. It was impossible to forget he was there. Over and over she found herself stopping to listen for the click of the tools on his belt when he shifted, the curses he muttered under his breath when he hit a snag, the whisper of his clothing as he walked. Somehow, the fact that they were in different rooms only made her more aware of him.

And she knew when he walked in even before he spoke.

"Okay, those are done. Where are the others?"

She rose to meet him. "There's the door on the guest room."

"Where's that?"

"Upstairs. And Josh's bathroom door."

"Upstairs?"

"Yes."

"Anything else on this floor?"

She hesitated. "The closet."

"The closet where?"

"My bedroom. The master bedroom," she corrected, feeling her cheeks warm.

A slow smile spread across Roberto's face. "Is that so? Does that mean I get the tour?"

She scowled at him. "I thought you were a professional."

"At some things." He eyed her. "At others, I like to think of myself as a dedicated amateur."

Her pulse beat a little harder. "The other two rooms are right next to each other."

"Might as well take care of this one first, since it's close." He picked up his toolbox. "Show me where it's at."

"You'll find it at the end of the hall."

"Oh, I think you'd better show me. A door that important, you'll want to get it done just right."

When she still hesitated, he grinned. "Relax, *chica.* It might shock you, but at thirty-nine I think I can just about manage to keep from tearing your clothes off and having my way with you at the sight of a bed. Not that the idea doesn't have its appeal," he added softly, the smile fading.

Frannie started down the hall, vividly aware of Roberto just behind her. Naked, on the bed, twined together. Would it be so hard to block the image if she hadn't been with him before? If she didn't remember the feel of his bare skin pressed to hers? They hadn't made love in a bed, but on the soft grass beneath the red oaks, with the rolling hills all around. And when he'd parted the front of her shirt to find her, he'd shown her just how electric touch could be.

The rooms opening onto the hallway were all closed off, leaving it dim, intimate. The door to her bedroom seemed very far away. And when they finally reached it, her hand on the knob was slippery with nerves. She opened it and they walked into a flood of light.

Soft blue walls, a cathedral ceiling, French doors leading to the pool deck. A half acre of pale gold carpet.

And a bed the size of Rhode Island.

He was being punished for boasting, Roberto thought. He was being made to suffer, because when it came down to it, he wasn't so far above it after all. What he was was full of it, because when he stood next to that wide swath of coverlet and pillows, all he could think about was having her naked beneath him, pressing her into the soft mattress and taking them both where he knew they could go.

"This is the door," Frannie said.

It was her hair that was the problem. He'd about flipped when he'd seen her come walking up with that sunbeam hair cut away into a little cap that made her look about sixteen and lighthearted and happy. All of a sudden, those delicate features weren't weighed down by the heavy spill of hair anymore. He could really see her again, chin and cheekbones, that delicious mouth that always spoke to him of mischief.

And tempted him to the point of madness.

Roberto set down the toolbox and pulled open the closet door.

It was his second mistake.

The closet was hers, he could tell the minute the door started to swing back and her scent flowed out to envelop him. The ranks of clothing whispered of her. There was a robe hanging from a hook on the back of the door. Red silk.

He swore he could smell his synapses frying.

Don't think about it, he told himself as he knelt next to the doorjamb and unscrewed the strike plate.

It was a simple repair that should have taken five minutes, but it seemed like it took him three or four times that because he couldn't focus. His eyes were on the wood and metal, but his attention was on Frannie.

She moved restlessly around the room, the way he imagined she might at night as she was getting undressed, slipping out of her shoes, unzipping her dress, sliding into that silky robe. Maybe she'd sit on the padded bench in her dressing area as she took off her jewelry. And he'd come up behind her and slide the robe off her shoulders to find her warm and naked and—

"How do you do that?"

The words brought him back to reality with a jolt. He blinked. "How do I…"

"How do you fix the door?"

He gave a sigh of relief. "Oh, that. See this hole?" He held up the strike plate, waggling his thumb in the gap. "The spring latch on the door is supposed to fit into it. In your doors, the strike plate's set too far into the jamb so that the latch never makes it that far."

"So how do you fix it?"

"Take it off and use a file to take away enough metal that the spring latch can make it in." He rose. "Where's your trash can?"

"In the dressing area," she said.

He walked through the threshold and in a flash took in the first room in the house that seemed truly hers. With its half wall of mirrors, deeply female furnishings and sense of luxurious disorder, it evoked the feel of a harem. On the polished wood counter, a hairbrush lay next to a bin of lipsticks and eye color. Within a wooden box with the top askew, he glimpsed the flash of gold. A deep blue silk scarf had been tossed over the padded stool as though she'd just taken it off. Her scent hovered in the air.

He saw painted porcelain sinks and gleaming fixtures. And in the far corner, next to a wall of glass brick, an enormous, unabashedly decadent tub big enough for two.

Soap, wet bodies, skin sliding over slippery skin.

That was it, Roberto thought. He gave in. A man could only take so much temptation, no matter how adult he was, and if he didn't get outside quick, his brain was going to go on overload. Forget the wastebasket, he'd file the strike plate in the garage. Better yet, he'd take it back to his place. He wheeled around abruptly.

It was his third mistake.

Because she was there, just behind him. They collided, and in the confusion he reached out to clutch her arms to keep her from falling.

Too bad he already had.

And with a low curse, he dragged her to him, crushed her lips to his and plunged them both into a hot madness.

It was nothing like their previous kiss. This time, there was no quiet exploration, no gentleness. This kiss was about heat and urgency. It was about the accumulated frustration of the past days, the need that pounded through him until it became all he was about. Her mouth was hot and avid against his and he drove her lips apart to taste her. Her body was lithe and he learned it anew with his hands. It was urgent, it was heedless and she matched him demand for demand. When he slid his hand up over her breast, the low moan in her throat very nearly drove him over the edge.

He was like a junkie getting his first taste after being on the wagon. He could feel the rush of her buzzing through his veins, intoxicating him, making him almost dizzy with it.

And like a junkie mainlining again, all he wanted was more.

The bed was there, mere feet away. All he had to do was walk over to it and lay her down. It was meant to happen. Why else would they have wound up together in this room if not for this? They were adults, they were both free. With all they had gone through, didn't they deserve it? Didn't they deserve the pleasure that they could give each other?

He heard her moan again and his body tightened. He felt her fingers slide up into his hair and he dragged them both deeper. He savored her mouth, let his lips press a tortured line down the smooth column of her throat, inhaled her scent. It had gone beyond want, now, beyond need, beyond choice and into the realm of compulsion.

Frannie couldn't catch a breath, didn't care. For that moment, she let the rush of sensation sweep her away into the heat and thunder, flash and fire. Twenty years before, she'd given him a playful kiss one afternoon at the end of a game of tag. It had sent little fizzes of excitement bubbling through her, but nothing compared to the way she'd felt days later when they'd finally made love. And now, history was repeating itself. That first brushing kiss at his place had ignited a slow burn in her that she couldn't ignore. But this, this was like gasoline thrown on fire.

She could feel the urgency, taste it even as she tasted him. His hands ran down her back, molding them together. Their mouths fused and she reveled in his touch, his scent, his taste, gloried in the pleasure that he drew forth from her with hands and lips and tongue. For years, she'd been deadened, but now under his touch she'd come alive.

It wasn't enough, Roberto knew it. It wasn't enough and yet he couldn't let himself take more. He heard Frannie's soft sigh of surrender, knew the exact moment that he could have taken her further, slipping off her dress, pressing her back on the bed. And maybe, caught up in the moment, she wouldn't have blamed him.

But he would have blamed himself.

So he stayed put, fought to pull back, fought to regain control. Fought finally to release her.

And watched as her eyes cleared.

They stared at each other, wordless.

She dragged her hands through her hair. "I must be out of my mind."

"Try to tell me that's just a complication," he challenged.

Frannie tried to slow her breath. "Try to tell me it's not."

"Don't pretend you haven't been thinking about it, because I don't buy it."

"Of course I've been thinking about it. But that doesn't mean I'm ready for it." She stepped away and whirled around to him. "What do you want from me, Roberto? I'm still trying to figure out how the pieces all fit together. I keep telling you I can't deal with this right now, and you won't listen."

"Yeah? That's because I didn't exactly notice you fighting me off just now." He clasped his hands together on top of his head, squeezed his eyes closed briefly and let out a long breath. "I shouldn't have said that. I'm sorry. I didn't intend for this to happen any more than you did. But there's something there between us or it wouldn't have."

She nodded slowly. "Then maybe we should stay away from each other so it doesn't happen again."

"Do you really think that's possible?"

It was her turn to be frustrated. "I don't know. Right now, I'm making this up as I go along. I do want you, Roberto, I admit it. I want you so much sometimes that I can't breathe. And it scares the hell out of me."

He didn't reply right away. "*Querida*," he said finally. "I can only imagine what you went through with that man. I'm not ignoring you. I get that you don't want to be involved right now after everything you've been through, but like I said before, I'm not Lloyd. At some point you're going to have to trust that. At some point you're going to have to trust yourself and listen to your heart."

"How am I supposed to listen to my heart if all I can hear is you telling me what you want me to do?" she fired back. "Give me—"

There was the sound of the door and giggling at the front of the house. "Anybody home?"

Frannie jerked away as though she'd been electrified. "Josh and Lyndsey," she hissed. "Be right out, honey," she said more loudly, smoothing down her dress and moving toward the door.

"Frannie." He waited until she turned. "You can hold back all you want, but we both know that's not going to make it go away. It's still there between us. Sooner or later you're going to have to deal with it."

"I know," she whispered.

And she walked out the door.

Chapter Nine

Roberto put a coin into the self-serve car wash. In Denver, he had a car wash at his company's facility to serve their fleet, as well as a gas pump. At least last time he'd checked. A man couldn't run a business for long when he was a thousand miles away. So far, between the Internet, his cell phone and his job-site managers pitching in, he'd done okay, but that wasn't likely to last too much longer. Especially with the economy, he needed to be there in person.

But how could he leave Red Rock now with everything that was going on with his family, Lloyd's murder, the fires and Frannie?

Above all, with Frannie.

He hadn't come so close to winning her back only to walk away, especially when she was still in peril. Until things settled down with her, he wasn't going anywhere.

He twisted the knob on the dial to wash and squeezed the trigger on the wand. Instantly, a jet of soap sprayed out over the dusty side of his truck, dripping onto the wet concrete below. It didn't seem to matter where in Texas he was, the dust just naturally found him. He moved around in a slow circle, from back to front, until soap was running down the paint.

And suddenly the water turned off.

"What the…" He looked behind him to see McCaskill with his hand on the control box and Wheeler just standing there, studying him with those washed-out blue eyes.

"Now you're going to tell me I'm not allowed to wash my car?" Roberto asked.

McCaskill propped one hand on the cinder block wall. "Nope, we just saw you here as we were driving by—thought you looked lonely."

"Feel free to grab a rag and pitch in."

"Pitch in. Hey, that's a good one, huh, Len?"

Wheeler didn't look amused. "I hear you been asking questions."

"No law against that."

"When it comes to police work, yeah, actually, there is. It's called obstructing an investigation."

"I'm not obstructing anything. I'm just having conversations with people."

"Oh, yeah? Cindy Fortune didn't seem to think so. I believe she used the word interrogation."

Roberto closed his eyes and gave a mental curse. "And you and I both know just how trustworthy Cindy Fortune's word about anything is."

"In this case, I'm inclined to believe her," Wheeler drawled. "We're in the middle of an investigation here,

Mendoza. We don't need you interfering and getting citizens all riled up."

Roberto leaned the wand up against the cinder block wall. "And here I thought you were worried about finding out who killed Lloyd Fredericks, not keeping the citizens calm."

"Actually, Mr. Mendoza, we worry about both."

"I'll keep that in mind."

"Good. Because if you keep on having any more of those conversations, we might just wind up having a conversation with you—in a jail cell."

McCaskill leaned forward and smiled. "Right next to your girlfriend."

Roberto felt a flare of anxiety go through him. "My girlfriend?"

"Frannie Fredericks," Wheeler clarified. "The woman still officially charged with the murder of Lloyd Fredericks. You two been spending a lot of time together, haven't you? For a couple of people who just knew one another casually twenty years ago, I mean."

"She hired me to repair her house."

"From what I can see, you been fixing an awful lot for her. Garage doors, roof, walls, finding the murder weapon dropped by some mysterious figure no one else seems to have seen…" Those pale blue eyes studied him. "You help her fix anything else, Mendoza? Like her husband?"

It felt like ice going down his spine. Ignore it, Roberto told himself. They were fishing, nothing more. "Give me a break, Wheeler. You took my fingerprints and my blood when I was in for questioning. If that had matched up with any other forensic evidence, you'd have slapped me in a cell in a heartbeat. Same thing with Frannie. You don't have anything and we both know it."

"Until we do, we're happy to go with obstructing an investigation," McCaskill put in.

"Only if you can prove I was obstructing."

"I'm not going to dance around with you anymore on this, Mendoza," Wheeler interrupted. "Stay out of this investigation or we'll have both you and Frannie Fredericks back in."

"Based on what? She hasn't been asking questions, I have."

Wheeler's eyes chilled. "Stay out of it. And if you're smart, you'll keep your distance from her, too. I don't like having an open homicide in my town. I want this cleaned up, and the quicker you get out of it, the quicker it will be."

McCaskill swiped a finger down the side of the truck. "You'd better get to rinsing," he said over his shoulder as they walked away. "You let the soap dry on your paint, it'll wreck the finish."

Frannie had always loved weddings. Maybe it was irrational, given how miserably her own marriage had turned out, but there was something about the optimism of two people pledging their lives to each other that had always made it easier for her to get through the day. And the next day. And the next.

White satin, lily of the valley, flower girls meandering down the aisle. Even watching the bride and groom wandering around the reception never failed to make her smile.

At least most days.

"Congratulations, you two," she told her cousin

Nicholas Fortune and his bride as they stopped at her table. "Or congratulations to you, Nick. The bride's supposed to get best wishes."

"Forget that." Charlene Fortune, née London, threaded her arm through her husband's. "I deserve congratulations for bagging the confirmed bachelor."

"Hey, who proposed to who?" Nick countered. "Give me some credit for knowing a good thing when I see it. Or see her." He grinned.

"You do look kind of like you won the lottery," Frannie observed. "Both of you."

Clad in a flowing white gown with a garland of flowers in her auburn hair, Charlene had a glow that could have lit Manhattan. Around them, guests began tapping knives against their water glasses to create an ever-louder chorus of clinking.

"Listen to your guests and kiss the bride, Nicholas," Frannie told him.

"My pleasure," he replied, taking Charlene in his arms and dipping her back with a flourish to kiss her until everyone whooped.

Charlene was laughing as she came back up. "You loon," she said.

"You'd better get used to it," Nick told her. "You're stuck with me now."

"I think I can handle that. Kiss me again, just so I can make sure." When he did, she beamed. "Oh, I wish I could bottle this feeling and give some to everyone I know."

Maybe that was the allure of weddings, Frannie thought as they walked off, the hope that some of that giddy magic would rub off. Then again, what would she do if it did? Would she really have the courage to step out and take it?

Sooner or later you're going to have to deal with it.

Roberto made it sound so simple. He was so certain of what he wanted. That didn't mean that she was ready for it. It felt so right with him, but what if that was just sentiment talking, a mix of the excitement of their reunion and feelings from long ago?

Worse, what if it wasn't? What if it was real and she ruined it by diving in before she was emotionally ready to be a partner to anyone? Frannie sighed. When she sat down and thought about it, there were a whole host of good reasons to stay away from Roberto Mendoza.

And deep down inside, she knew it didn't matter. Over a week had passed since they'd kissed in her bed-room, over a week since she'd seen him. And every moment of every hour of every day in between, she'd wanted him. She'd tried to keep him at a distance, she'd tried to keep him out of her head. She should've realized at the start that it was impossible. And now, she didn't know what to do.

To distract herself, she brought out her camera and began to snap pictures: a little girl standing on her grandfather's feet, giggling as he sidestepped her around the dance floor, Nick's three black-haired goddaughters solemnly trading different-colored Jordan almonds from the favors, William Fortune sending Lily out for a twirl as they danced to Glenn Miller.

Frannie turned to frame up another shot and felt someone tap her on the shoulder.

"You're Frannie Fredericks, aren't you?" asked a stocky woman in heavy face makeup and a lime-green silk dress.

In the two weeks since her release from jail, Frannie

had become an expert at recognizing the varying reactions of strangers to Lloyd's murder. There were the sympathetic ones, the ones who looked at her with pity, the curious, the sincere. And the ones like this woman, the emotional vultures who just wanted a story to tell.

"It must have been horrible to have your husband murdered like that." The woman eyed her avidly. "And for it to be one of those Mendozas. After everything your family has done for them."

Frannie felt a stir of anger at the presumption. "If you're talking about Roberto Mendoza, he hasn't even been charged." She rose. "Excuse me."

As much as she was thrilled to see Nick and Charlene so happy, she was sick to death of the stares, the comments, the hissing whispers that cut off when she approached. She didn't feel like a guest so much as a target. The good thing about the camera was that it gave her both a shield and a reason to leave.

She snapped a picture of Ricky Faraday holding hands with his girlfriend while a couple of younger boys wrinkled their noses. Nearer by, Josh and Lyndsey worked their way through the tables. He was introducing her to the relatives, Frannie saw. And Lyndsey was taking pains to shake hands and talk with each and every one of them. First Josh's clothes, now his family.

"It's so nice to meet you," Frannie heard her say to Emmett Jamison, who with his wife, Linda, ran the Fortune Foundation. "Everyone speaks so highly of the work the Foundation does. I hope that someday I might be able to come to work there." She paused expectantly.

"Uh, yes, well, stop in sometime." Emmett cleared his throat. "See what we're doing."

Lyndsey blushed becomingly. "Oh, could I?"

Maybe she was just being an overprotective mother, Frannie thought resignedly. Maybe it came from having only one child. Everyone else seemed to like Lyndsey; Josh thought he loved her. Frannie focused and squeezed off a sequence of shots of Josh leading Lyndsey onto the dance floor. It would make a good gift for the girl. A peace offering, perhaps. It was looking more and more like Lyndsey was going to be around for the long term. And Frannie supposed as she skirted a table at the edge of the room, it was past time for her to get used to it.

"She had blood all over her, I heard," someone said nearby, *sotto voce*. Frannie glanced over to see an older woman with short, gray hair leaning over to her companion. "And that Roberto Mendoza just walking the streets as big as life."

Frannie felt the flare of anger.

"You know, everything was fine until he came back," the woman's friend said. "Now we've got fires and murder and all sorts of things."

"I heard he left in the first place because he had to," the gray-haired woman replied.

Her friend nodded sagely. "Trouble with the law, someone said. I just hope they hurry up with the trial and put that murderer away for good."

Lies, complete fabrications, character assassination, Frannie thought as she walked past. An image of Roberto filled her mind—his strength, his unquestioning acceptance—and she stopped and spun back to the pair.

"Well, since I'm the only one who's been charged with the murder so far, I'm personally hoping the trial doesn't happen for a long, long time. Of course, maybe you have evidence the police don't. Smile." The pair gaped at her and she snapped a picture of them. "What a lovely photo of your fillings. Thank you," she sang, and turned away.

She was instantly sorry. "Frannie, Frannie, Frannie, you ought to be ashamed of yourself," she muttered under her breath, shaking her head.

"You think so?" a voice asked. "Here I was just about to applaud you."

Frannie turned to see Gloria Fortune, the wife of her cousin Jack. And the sister of Roberto. "Oh, Gloria, they're driving me crazy."

"You? Five more minutes of this and *I'm* going to be the one in jail for homicide."

"Oh, take down the one in the lime-green," Frannie begged. "I want to watch."

Gloria rolled her eyes, her honey-brown hair rippling. "I don't know whether to laugh or cry. But what am I doing complaining to you?"

"Who better?"

"You know he didn't do it, Frannie, right?"

"Of course I know it. What drives me crazy is that no one else in town seems to. They never even arrested him and everyone's got him convicted. It's not fair," she said in frustration. "He deserves better."

She glanced up and caught Gloria looking at her searchingly.

"You seem to have thought about this," Gloria commented. "I didn't realize you were such a fan of Roberto."

"He and I—I just don't think it's right," she said lamely.

And for no reason she could figure, Gloria suddenly

gave a broad smile. "Me, either," she said, reaching out to tuck Frannie's arm through hers. "Tell me more about yourself, Frannie. I think it's time we get to know each other better."

"The young stock looks good."

Roberto and his uncle Ruben walked along the paddock behind the barn at the Double Crown. Roberto had come out to the ranch because he'd been too restless to sit still. There was anger at McCaskill and Wheeler, frustration that after two weeks of asking questions, he knew no more than when he'd started. But most of all, there was Frannie.

"Five colts and seven fillies," Ruben Mendoza said in satisfaction. "They're coming along. We're going to start gentling them." He glanced at Roberto. "You could come out and help with the halter training and getting them used to grooming. I'm too old to lean over and pick up their feet."

"*Tío* Ruben, when are you going to retire?" Roberto stopped to lean on the white railing. A brown mare and her filly walked over, ears pricked.

"I tried retiring," Ruben said, pulling out his pocket knife to quarter one of the apples he habitually carried in his pockets. "Your *Tía* Rosita threatened to brain me with a frying pan."

Roberto watched his uncle feed the mare some apple and reached out for one of the pieces. "That didn't have anything to do with you sneaking her fresh *churros,* did it? You know how she gets about those."

"I have made foolish mistakes in my time, but none so foolish as that. She said I was underfoot. The truth is, I was happy to retire from being retired. And now she has her days at the house, I have my days out here, and all is pleasant." He clapped a hand on Roberto's shoulder. "I will tell you a secret, Robertito. A man can only be as happy as the woman in his life."

Didn't he know it. He hadn't talked to Frannie since the afternoon he'd held her in his arms. And he hadn't stopped thinking about her once. He'd had everything in that moment, all he wanted, heated and gasping against him, and he'd pulled back. He'd been crazy, Roberto thought. Except that deep down he'd known he hadn't had everything. He'd had her body, not her mind.

There were parts of him that didn't seem to get it, though. Morning after morning, he awoke from tumultuous dreams of her, tense from arousal with no outlet, desire settled in his belly like a load of rocks.

He hadn't stopped wanting her once.

"The question is, how do you make them happy?" he asked aloud. The filly poked her muzzle through the slats in the fence, and Roberto held out the apple on the flat of his palm for her to lip up and crunch.

Ruben eyed him. "A young *caballero* like you, I think you would know."

Roberto snorted. "The more I know about women, the more I realize I don't know anything at all."

"Ahh, I understand. The question is not how do you make women happy, the question is how do you make *a* woman happy. A special woman, no?" Ruben turned toward the bar with a half smile on his face. "For that, we must go to my office."

Roberto gave him a dubious look. "Why, do you have a handbook there?"

"Better, *caballero*. A bottle of tequila."

"Now that might just—" Roberto began and stopped short. Frannie rode around the corner from the barnyard on a chestnut mare. She pulled up when she saw him.

He stared at her. The breeze tossed her hair a bit. There was about her a flavor of wildness he couldn't identify. Something kinetic surged between them then, something he had no words for, but that sent the adrenaline rocketing through his veins. The seconds stretched out.

And then she wheeled the mare around and rode out of the barnyard like the hounds of hell were behind her.

Roberto stood, watching without moving, barely registering the fact that his uncle was speaking as the hoofbeats faded. He stirred, and shook his head. "I'm sorry, *Tío* Ruben, what?"

Ruben gave him a shrewd glance. "I asked if you wanted to borrow a horse."

Chapter Ten

Frannie crouched over Daisy's withers. She'd had enough. She'd had enough of the sudden silences, the false condolences and outrage of strangers who assumed Roberto had killed Lloyd. She'd given up trying to explain, sick of the way they looked at her, perplexed, as though understanding the facts wasn't nearly as important as having a target to blame. It had taken every last bit of her patience to stay to the end of the wedding.

And now, she wanted to wipe it all away.

She needed speed, she needed the wind in her hair, the vibration of hooves on the ground.

She needed Roberto.

"Come on, girl," she urged Daisy as the mare galloped along. Frannie knew where they were going. Even two decades hadn't wiped the memory away. Out through the rolling countryside toward the afternoon sun that hung low in the sky. Daisy picked her way down an embankment to cross the little stream that wound through the Double Crown, then Frannie urged her on, faster, to the place that lay waiting. They followed the trail straight up the side of the hill to the red oaks, the trail she hadn't used in years. Nineteen of them. And then they were at the top, out of breath.

Blue sky, a soft breeze and the almost-liquid rippling of the grass over the hillsides. This was what she'd needed—this sense that she'd escaped from all that dogged her, that she'd left it all behind back at the ranch house. Here, she was just Frannie, with no fears, no responsibilities, no threats—just open space and silence.

And then she heard the sound of hooves.

She'd been certain he would come, from the moment she'd seen him in the barnyard. She hadn't come to the ranch expecting him to be there, and yet the sight of his truck had come as no surprise. In some strange way, it was as though she'd known in her bones she would see him. And she'd known in her bones that he'd follow.

Roberto rode up over the edge of the escarpment. There were no words spoken, no smile, as he reined his horse in. Intensity shimmered around him. He slid out of the saddle, and Frannie began walking toward him. He took a step, then two, and then they were running toward each other across the gap.

The next instant, they were in each other's arms, pressed together so tightly she almost couldn't breathe, and yet she didn't want him to stop because it meant giving up this reality, this contact, this connection, the utter rightness of the two of them together in this place at this moment.

His mouth on hers was like a benediction and the

words for what she felt were "now," and "finally," and "yes." She feasted on him like a woman starving. Her hands cradled his face. And then she was sliding her arms around him, tugging his shirt out of his jeans so that she could run her hands up underneath and feel his skin, finally, his skin against her palms.

It was unimaginable that she'd waited, impossible now to understand how or why she'd held back, when all she wanted was to devour him. The world reduced to touch and taste and sound: the feel of his hands roaming over her body, the dark male flavor of him, the rapid-fire clatter of snaps as she ripped his shirt open. Pleasure layered upon pleasure, touch upon touch.

With a sound of impatience, Roberto shrugged off his shirt. He caught the bottom of her tank top in his hands, stripping it off over her head with a suddenness that took her breath. For an instant, she stood before him, bare breasted. Then they came together, and the heat and the feel of his naked chest against the sensitive skin of her breasts made her moan aloud. How could they have spent so many years apart when the thought of separating for even a moment to pull off their boots seemed unendurable? They divided, they rejoined. And open mouth to open mouth, they lowered down to the grass as one.

Roberto unsnapped her jeans and tugged them down her thighs. She lay back on the grass and their discarded shirts, hair tousled, eyes slumberous, wearing only a scrap of black lace around her hips. He trailed fingers down over the long line of her body. "Frannie," he whispered in something close to awe.

And she was long and lovely and luminous, the

unformed lines of girlhood turned to the sweeping curves of woman. And she was more beautiful, more desirable as an adult than she'd ever been as a girl. There was magic to her and mystery and a sort of hypnotic secret that came only from woman.

How many times had he dreamed of this, how many nights had he woken alone in the darkness, body soaked with sweat, lips still heated from the memory of hers, knowing, knowing above all else that they belonged together, that she was the only one?

And knowing that it was impossible.

To have her now in his arms, warm and willing, silky and fragrant against him, was more than he could ever have dreamed. It took him beyond simple desire into a kind of delirious joy. And when he stripped off the rest of his clothes and lay down next to her again, it was as though some tone had been sounded in his deepest soul, as pure as the ringing of a crystal goblet, a sound for which the words were "yes" and "this is it," the certainty that he'd found the one true thing.

Frannie gasped at the feel of his hands sliding over her body. How many times over the years had she wondered? How many times had she told herself that she just wasn't made for sex, that Lloyd was right—she was frigid? It was her, always something wrong with her that she couldn't respond to the impatient gropings of his hands, the awkward explorations that never worked because he never bothered to understand how it felt, and what she liked and what aroused her.

All that was gone because he didn't matter, none of it mattered. It wasn't about thinking when Roberto touched her. It was only about sensation, reaction, the same way a flame burned without knowing how or why.

He slid his hand up over her breasts and she arched against him, moaning incoherently as sensation ricocheted through her. And all she wanted was more because it wasn't enough, could never be enough. There weren't enough hours in her life for her to feel the roughness of his palm slip over her breasts, to feel those clever, clever fingers turn her nipples to hard peaks. And yet this was just the beginning; she knew there was more.

She remembered.

He traced his tongue down her throat to her breasts. The teasing trail dragged a moan from her. When he fastened his mouth over her nipple, coherent thought simply deserted her. She jolted, crying out, pressing against him, wanting, needing to move, to explore, yet utterly overwhelmed by the overlapping sensations of mouth and lips and tongue, by his hand tormenting her other breast. It was too much, but not enough. She burned for more.

As though he'd heard her thoughts, Roberto shifted to press kisses over the quivering flat of her belly. And Frannie was aware of precisely this: the soft grass beneath her, the warm trail of his tongue, the tension forming between her thighs, a slow curl of heat she barely recognized because it had been so long since she'd felt it.

With a sound of impatience, he hooked his fingers in the sides of her briefs, dragging them down and leaving her open to the heat of his breath. A shiver ran through her. Anticipation had her moving restlessly against him, clutching at the grass, his shoulders, anything.

Then he laid his mouth on her and she cried out. There was heat, the softness of his lips, the maddening swirl of his tongue as he caressed her and took her somewhere she hadn't been in so many years it should have been alien, and yet it was instantly familiar, this tension, this pressure, this bursting need. He took her to a world she'd soared in once, back before she'd known fear or defeat, a flight of ecstasy fueled by touch, her hips bucking against him until she was flung into free fall, shuddering and quaking, spiraling down from a great height into laughter and pure joy.

"Oh my, where have you been?" She kissed him wherever she could reach, half-giddy as he moved up over her.

"It doesn't matter. I'm here now."

But the tension had only been banked back, not vanquished. With his hands and his mouth he set her to trembling. When he moved up and over her, she wanted, she needed in a way she'd never dreamed possible. The setting sun behind him lit his hair with a penumbra of fire, shadowing his eyes, making him look like some primitive warrior.

"I need to be inside you," he ground out in what was half plea, half demand, and when he moved himself through that slick cleft between her thighs, searching for the spot, she held her breath in anticipation, shivering, feeling the ache, the need, the emptiness waiting to be filled.

"Please," she whispered.

Then he shifted and drove himself into her, and in one hot, slick rush they were coupled.

Her cry echoed his groan. For an instant they were

poised, staring into each other's eyes, their gazes locked together as intimately as their bodies. Roberto leaned in and pressed a kiss on her. *"Querida,"* he breathed against her lips.

And slowly, slowly he began to move.

There was no rush, no furious pounding. Instead, his strokes were measured, almost leisurely, taking him nearly all the way out of her, then back in slow and deep. But there was a sense of power banked back in each thrust, a sense of breathless expectation. His eyes burned black with arousal. His body trembled with the effort of control.

And it drove her mad with need.

Each slide of his flesh against hers made her shudder. Each slide took her higher. She clutched at his back, feeling the muscles clench and flow under her fingers as he moved faster. And gradually, gradually, he reached a rhythm, that rhythm, that ancient, timeless rhythm that was love and hope and renewal all in one.

And it was impossible—the tension, the exquisite rush of pleasure that swept through her with every stroke—impossible for her to bear it one more instant, impossible for it to end. She gasped for air, twisted against him, wrapped her legs around his waist. She cried out for more. And then the tension compressed all that need, and arousal and desire down into a single point, a single point that held for a shuddering instant before it suddenly exploded, bursting through her entire body, sending her jolting and crying out, clenching around him in mindless ecstasy.

And she heard his helpless groan as it put him over

the edge, as he drove into her one final time and spilled himself, pulling her hard against him.

Above them, one by one, the stars came out in the darkening sky.

He wasn't naive enough to think that perfect happiness existed, but if it did, it would have to feel something like this, Roberto thought as he lay beside Frannie, waiting for his heart rate to level.

She stirred. "If we stay out here too much longer, we're not going to be able to find our way back."

"Relax, there's a full moon tonight. Besides, the horses know how to find the barn."

She shifted to look at him. "How did you find this place again? It's been almost twenty years."

"I don't know. I didn't think about it." He hadn't, just mounted Barnabus, the gelding Ruben had given him, and gone on instinct. Or maybe it wasn't instinct. Maybe some part of him had a special sense for her and where she was. Maybe they were connected. It was a ridiculous thought, he knew it was ridiculous, but maybe a man was allowed to be ridiculous at a time like this.

Roberto laughed aloud.

Frannie turned her head toward him. "What's the joke?"

He shook his head a little. "Nothing. Life is good." He leaned over and pressed a kiss to her nose, and figured he'd kiss her cheek while he was there. And since her mouth was nearby, he might as well do that, and...

Long moments slipped away as hand smoothed over flesh, needs long denied built afresh. They touched, they demanded. Again they rose, again they fell. And this time when they finished, they stayed linked together and let themselves slip further into slumber.

The full moon overhead shone down, silvering the path before them as they rode up to the barn. Triggered by their motion, the flood lamps flicked on in the stable yard.

"Finally, light," Frannie said.

"I thought moonlight was supposed to be romantic."

"There's romantic and there's not being able to see where you're going." She stopped beyond the mounting block and slid down from the saddle, feeling the sweet ache between her thighs. "Lucky thing we found the road. Otherwise, we'd have been stuck out there all night."

Roberto gave her a lazy smile. "I can think of worse things than being left with nothing to do but make love with you until sunrise."

A shiver ran through her stomach. Still… "What would your uncle think if we'd come traipsing in tomorrow morning?"

"I doubt *Tío* Ruben would have been all that surprised. Hell, he was the one who gave me Barnabus to ride."

"He knew?"

"*Querida,* at this point, I'd say anyone who looks at us together for long will have a pretty good idea something's going on."

Like Lily, she thought. "Lily already warned me about being seen with you."

"Really?" His gaze sharpened. "When?"

Frannie led Daisy into the railed, U-shaped enclosure of the cross ties and turned the mare to face the front. "Last week, when I met her for lunch. Your name slipped out." She concentrated on swapping Daisy's bridle for her halter and clipping the lead lines onto either side.

"And she said stay away from that awful Mendoza boy?" His voice held not humor, but flickers of irritation.

"Lily isn't Cindy, Roberto. It's not about you as a person, it's the situation. My husband's dead, we've both been in jail for his murder, and now the two of us are involved? If that seems fast to me, how do you think it's going to look to everyone else?"

He ducked out of Barnabus' adjacent cross tie to face her. "If it was too fast, why did you come to the Double Crown?"

"I didn't know I'd find you here."

"But you rode out knowing I'd follow."

"Yes."

"Why?"

She turned to unfasten Daisy's cinch. "I'd think that would be obvious."

"Nothing's obvious here, Frannie, and nothing's simple. Are you getting cold feet about what we just did?"

"Yes. No. I don't know," she burst out. "How can I when all I want is for you to touch me again?"

His gaze heated. Electricity snapped between the two of them as he pulled her into his arms to fuse his mouth to hers. Desire and frustration, longing and hope. And fear. The emotions swirled around in the kiss, overlaying that always-present flare of arousal.

He released her. "Wheeler and McCaskill stopped by to see me today."

"What?" Head still spinning from the kiss, Frannie stared at him.

"It's all right. It wasn't about bringing either of us in.

But it's gotten back to them that I'm asking questions and they don't like it."

Daisy shifted impatiently. Focus on the details, Frannie reminded herself. She needed to focus on getting Daisy untacked and groomed and bedded down, not on things she couldn't change. She moved away from Roberto to pull off the saddle and set it on the rail. "I don't know why they care. It's not like they're coming up with any answers."

"No, but they take a dim view of people they think are interfering with their investigation." Roberto walked back to where Barnabus was crosstied.

"You're not interfering with anything."

"That's not how they see it."

Frannie picked up the dandy brush and began sweeping the dirt out of Daisy's coat in long strokes. "You talked to a few people, that's all." She stopped. "Isn't it?"

"Yes, and I told them that. I also told them that you weren't a part of any of it."

Her stomach tightened with anxiety. "Me? How did I come into it?"

"Either they're watching us or your mother told them. Or both."

"Cindy? I don't understand."

He let out a breath. "She stopped by when I was at your house, working on the garage door."

"She stopped by? When?" Irritation pricked her. "And when, exactly, were you planning to tell me about it?"

"I didn't think I had to. She told Josh to tell you—I assumed he had."

"He didn't." And there was too much going on all together. "What did she want?"

"I don't know. But she wasn't thrilled to see me. She apparently went to the cops and told them I was asking questions and got them all riled up."

Focus on the details. Frannie went back to brushing Daisy. "What did the detectives say?"

"They tried to threaten me with arrest, but they don't have any cause." Roberto hesitated. "When that didn't work, they made noises about bringing you in for violating the conditions of your release by talking to people involved in the case."

The brush dropped out of her suddenly nerveless fingers. "But I—"

"You haven't talked to anybody, Frannie, I know." He bent down to retrieve it. "And they know, too. It's an empty threat. They're just trying to scare us."

"They're doing a good job." It was starting again, that sense that everything was coming down at once, and she couldn't control any of it.

Swiftly, Roberto moved to her, put a hand to her cheek. "It's okay. They don't have anything on either of us or we'd be back in jail already."

"But that could change at any moment."

"Until they solve the murder, yes. The problem is, they also don't have anything on the case that we haven't given to them."

"What does that mean, we just wait?"

"We could. I can stop what I'm doing if you say so and leave it to your brother Ross. Or he and I could both stay out of it, which is what the cops want. I don't know that that's going to help us, though. The other possibility is that I keep asking questions and see if something bubbles up. It's your call—what do you want?"

"I want this done," she burst out, grabbing the saddle and bridle. "I want to stop worrying. I want to stop thinking about Josh and you and me being in trouble. I want to get on with my life." She strode toward the barn and the tack room.

He grabbed Barnabus' tack and followed. "That's the same thing I want."

"And do you really think what you're doing is likely to make that happen?"

"I don't know, to be honest. I'm not an investigator, I don't have experience to go by. But I do know people, and sometimes putting pressure in the right place can break something loose. To me, it's a chance worth taking. It's not just about me, though. I'm not going to do anything that might put you at risk unless you say it's okay."

It was too much, Frannie thought. It made her want to clap her hands over her ears, to run, to get far, far away from everyone and everything. And yet she knew that wasn't possible. Defiance stirred. "They could come get me at any time—I've known that from the day I got out. And I want it to stop. We've got to end this." She slapped on the barn lights and turned to him. "If you think there's even a chance that what you're doing will help, then keep at it."

"I think that's the right choice."

"There's a bigger issue here, though," she continued, "and that's the two of us. Lily was right, you and me being involved right now is a bad move. How do you think it's going to look to people if we start showing up around town together with Lloyd dead?"

"The police asked me about that, too," Roberto said. "The problem is, we are involved."

Frannie stepped into the tack room without responding and hung up the bridle.

He followed her inside. "Or are you talking about more than just staying out of the public eye?" he said.

"I think we need to keep our distance."

"This isn't about how it looks, is it?" Roberto asked, eyes steady on her. "It's about you backing away."

Temper flared. "I wanted what happened tonight. I still do—but it's not just about me, it's about this whole situation. We're not kids anymore. We have to do what's smart, Roberto. We have to be grown-ups. And right now, that means keeping this under wraps."

His jaw tightened. "And after?"

She took two swift steps toward him and pressed her mouth to his. The seconds went by and he felt the saddle slipping out of his hands.

She stepped back. "After, we'll see what happens."

Chapter Eleven

"What can I get for you?" Roberto asked, tossing down a couple of bar mats before the blonde in the red dress. Appropriate, he supposed, since she was here at Red.

She tossed her hair back. "My friends are going to have a margarita and a blueberry peach cobbler martini, and I'm going to try your PB&J martini."

A peanut butter and jelly martini. Roberto resisted the urge to roll his eyes as he reached for bottles and started mixing. Why people sucked down syrupy-sweet stuff and called it a cocktail was beyond him. If they didn't like the taste of alcohol, then why the hell drink it? And why try to pretend one of these concoctions was a martini when the only thing it had in common with the classic vodka and vermouth version was the shape of the glass?

But he didn't figure he had any business saying that to a customer, especially not one buying ten-dollar cocktails. It wasn't her fault he'd been a cranky SOB for the past week. To compensate, he dredged up a smile.

"Are you good?" purred the blonde.

"What?" Roberto blinked, his hands freezing in the midst of pouring the contents of the shaker into the martini glass.

"Are you good? At mixing drinks," the blonde added with a throaty laugh.

It took him a minute to realize she was coming on to him. Of course. And meanwhile, the one woman he wanted, the woman who made it impossible for him to think, to sleep, he couldn't get near.

"I don't know, you tell me." Roberto set the martini on the bar mat before the blonde.

"It sounds like an invitation," she said, lifting up the glass to take a drink. "Mmm. Well, if you're this good at cocktails, I can hardly wait to see more."

The door from the outside opened. "—just have one drink and go," said a female voice. He glanced up out of habit to see two or three women walking in. And then everything seemed to stop for a moment.

Because with them was Frannie.

Adrenaline surged through his veins. Seven days had passed since they'd been together, seven days during which he hadn't touched her, hadn't seen her, hadn't even talked to her. Seven days during which all he'd done was want. And now, she was here, just across the room from him, so close and yet achingly far away.

"—you think?" The blonde was staring at him, obviously looking for an answer.

Roberto brought himself back. "What?"

She slid her fingers down the stem of her glass. "I

said, maybe I ought to come back near closing time and order myself another martini."

He put the other two drinks up on the bar and cashed out her tab. "Yeah, sure, there will be someone tending bar until eleven. Excuse me."

He moved to fill orders for one of the waitresses, but he was really only watching Frannie and her friends walk across the bar to cluster around a small table. Mechanically, he mixed drinks, grateful for the practice he'd gotten over the previous three months. It allowed his hands to keep moving while every bit of his attention was bent on her.

She slid onto one of the high bar chairs, shrugging off her purse and catching the strap as it hit her wrist so that she could hook it over the chair back. There was something unconsciously graceful and innately feminine about the gesture. Roberto snorted at himself as he opened a beer. This was how bad he'd gotten—even watching her take off her purse knocked him over.

And then she glanced up and caught his eye and it took him a second or two to remember how to breathe.

Fate's timing sucked. It had taken years, but they'd finally found each other again. They'd reconnected, slowly, but surely. For one incredible night, Frannie had overcome her fears and they'd glimpsed what they could be together.

Then the specter of Lloyd's murder had arisen and now the only thing more impossible than staying away from her was going to her. Silently, he damned Lloyd Fredericks. But damning him wasn't going to help anything. What was going to help was finding the murderer and putting this whole mess to rest.

Roberto caught Frannie's eye again. Putting a shot glass on the counter, he poured in some tequila then cut his gaze and focused on the glass.

He didn't have to do it twice. "I'll get the drinks," he heard her tell her friends.

Then she was walking over to him and all he could do was watch and imagine for just that moment how it would be if she were coming to him for real. She wore a dress that swirled around her calves and left her arms bare, a dress the exact blue of her eyes. Her sunbeam hair gleamed.

She stopped before him and rested her hands on the polished wood of the bar. He found himself fascinated by the beat of her pulse in her throat. "How are you?" he asked.

"I'm good. How about you?"

"Just now? Perfect." A wisp of her scent reached him and that quickly he was catapulted back to those moments under the red oaks when he'd held her in his arms. He could taste her lips, feel her soft skin, hear the whisper of the grass in the breeze.

Her fingers were right there, inches from his as he tossed down the bar napkins. His mouth went dry with want. What was the harm in touching her? It would take so little to reach out, lay his hand over hers just for a second. Instead, he rested it on the edge of the wood and looked his fill.

"You're beautiful," he said.

She flushed. "I want to order drinks."

"I want you."

The quiet words vibrated in the air. For a beat, neither moved. Desire surged between them like a physical thing.

Frannie moistened her lips. "You should be careful. Someone could hear you."

There was a burst of laughter from a group farther down the bar. "Unlikely, but never mind. What can I get you?"

"I'll have a mojito, plus a Dos Equis and two frozen margaritas for my friends."

"Salt?"

"One with, one without."

"Coming up." He added margarita mix, tequila and ice to a blender and flipped it on.

"Have you found anything out?" she asked.

"Nothing noteworthy so far. I'm going to go see Lyndsey tomorrow." He poured the margaritas into glasses. "She might know something about what Josh did at the Spring Fling. I'll let you know what I find out."

"Good luck."

"I need it. It's driving me crazy that I can't find someone else, anyone else, who saw that guy who tossed away the crowbar. I need a way to convince the cops he's real. If I only had—" He stopped, staring down at the mint leaves he was muddling for Frannie's mojito. Like he'd been muddled, he realized suddenly. "We've been missing a bet."

"What do you mean?"

"Your camera. You always take it with you places. Did you have it with you at the Spring Fling?"

"Of course. I took three or four rolls of film before everything happened."

"Have you gone through them?"

"No." She smiled faintly. "I've been busy. I did get them developed, though."

"Good. We should go through them, see if we notice anything unusual. Maybe we'll find a picture of the guy, or catch Lloyd talking to someone."

"It's kind of a long shot."

"True. Then again, what have we got to lose? Let's at least go through them." He placed her mojito before her and set the other drinks beside it. "I could come over to your house."

"Do you think that's smart?"

"Do you care?"

Her eyes darkened. "No."

"Good. Then when?"

"Tomorrow night after it gets dark, maybe nine or ten. Josh is going to the ball game with Lyndsey. His curfew isn't until midnight. We should have plenty of time."

"To having plenty of time." Roberto picked up the shot of tequila, clicked it unobtrusively on her mojito glass and downed it.

"I'll see you there." She filled her hands with drinks.

"I'll see you in my dreams."

Lyndsey Pollack lived with her mother on the north side of town in a tired-looking neighborhood that had probably been old already when Eisenhower was president. There was no guard shack here, just sidewalks cracked by tree roots and lawns sporting foreclosure signs.

The Pollackses' small ranch could have used a few gallons of paint, Roberto thought as he studied the flaking stucco around the doorbell. There was no response when he pressed the button.

The red car he'd seen his first day at Frannie's was

in the drive, but the shades on the house were still drawn. He checked his watch. Ten-thirty. He rang the bell again and waited. He'd hoped to stop by early enough to catch Lyndsey before she lit out for the day, but maybe he'd missed her. Or maybe she was just a late sleeper.

He was reaching out for the bell one last time when he heard the noise of a dead bolt being drawn and the door opened a few inches.

"Jeez, chill out, already. There are people sleeping." Lyndsey peered out at him. "Who are you?"

"Roberto Mendoza. I was the guy working on the doors over at Josh Fredericks' house last week."

"Oh, yeah." She hesitated. "What do you want?"

"I was hoping we could talk for a couple minutes."

"About what?"

"About Josh and the Spring Fling."

She was already shaking her head before he even finished. "No thank—"

He put out his hand to block the closing door. "Wait."

Something in her eyes hardened. "Look, mister, I don't know you. You keep up like this, I'm going to call the cops." She reached in her pocket and pulled out a cell phone.

"The cops are precisely what I'm trying to avoid. Hear me out for five minutes. For Josh's sake."

It stopped her, as he'd intended. "What are you talking about?"

"Let me in and I'll tell you."

She studied him a minute, chewing on her lip. Even though she was seventeen, her face still held some of the unformed roundness of childhood. "Okay," she said finally, "but we'll have to keep it down. My mom's sleeping. She works the night shift."

"Whatever you say."

The house was smaller than it looked from the outside. Over the fireplace directly opposite the door hung a convex mirror with metallic rays coming off it. The sunlight streaming in through the back windows showed the worn spots on the carpet.

"Let's go into the kitchen," Lyndsey said, turning through a swinging door. "We'll make less noise there."

If the neighborhood looked like it was from the fifties, the kitchen was more a relic of the seventies with avocado appliances and maple veneer cabinets.

"You can sit over there." She nodded at a vintage dinette set. It was another seventies relic with a faux woodgrain top and a quartet of swiveling vinyl chairs. A stack of mail and a dirty cereal bowl sat to one side; a sweatshirt draped over the back of one of the chairs. Or not a sweatshirt, Roberto realized, looking closer. A black hoodie.

"Isn't it a little warm for sweatshirts?"

"What? Oh, that's Josh's," she said dismissively, digging a Coke out of the refrigerator. "He left it last time he was here." She cracked open the can and took a swallow. "All right, so talk. That's what you wanted, right?"

What he wanted was to take a good close look at the hoodie, but he supposed it would be a useless exercise. If it had been the one Josh had worn the night of the Spring Fling, he would have washed it. Assuming he'd gotten anything on it. Pure speculation, Roberto told himself. Then again…

"You were at the Spring Fling with Josh, right?"

"Yeah."

"What did you do?"

"Walked around, went on some rides. Ate corndogs." Lyndsey didn't bother to sit, but leaned against the counter.

"How did he seem? Did he act funny?"

"What do you mean, funny?" She tucked a strand of hair behind her ear. "You said something about Josh and the cops. What, is he in trouble? Like he had something to do with his dad getting killed?"

"Did he?"

"No way. Why would he have done that?"

"Things happen. Besides, from what I hear Lloyd Fredericks was putting up a pretty stiff fight to split the two of you up."

"Yeah? So? It made Josh mad—it made me mad—but you don't kill a guy over that."

"Someone killed him over something."

"Well, it wasn't Josh," she flared, thumping her Coke down angrily.

"How do you know?"

"Because I know Josh. Besides, I was with him."

"The whole night? Were you there when he fought with Lloyd?"

She opened her mouth, then closed it. "I had to go home a little early. I had this sinus thing."

"When did you leave?"

"Nine-thirty, ten. But I don't know anything about a fight."

She was lying, he thought. "That's funny, because it happened around nine. There were witnesses. People heard it."

A trapped look flashed over her face. "Maybe I had the time wrong. I don't remember."

"If you saw anything at all, if he said anything, you need to tell me."

"Josh wouldn't…you don't… I can't talk to you about this." Abruptly she seemed near tears. "You have to go."

"If you care about Josh, you'll tell me what you know."

Wordlessly, she walked to the door.

Roberto waited a moment, then followed. At the threshold, he stopped. "Here's one of my cards. It's got my cell phone number on it. If you change your mind and want to talk, call me."

She took the card, but didn't look at it. Instead, she watched him walk out the door and step to the edge of the porch.

"Hey, mister."

Roberto turned back to her.

Lyndsey hesitated. "Lloyd Fredericks was a bad person. Whoever killed him did us all a favor."

Half a loaf was better than none. It was the mantra that had helped Frannie survive. Every time life with Lloyd had become intolerable over the years, she'd looked at Josh and reminded herself that maybe she couldn't have it all, but she had a lot. And it had gotten her through.

But it hadn't helped the previous evening at Red. It hadn't helped at all. She'd been with Roberto and yet not. She'd spoken to him, but only briefly, unable to say anything she really wanted to. She'd seen him, but only in carefully rationed glances, cautious not to give herself away. And she'd stood for an excruciating few moments with her hand mere inches from his, almost vibrating with the need to touch.

Walking out that door after only half a loaf had been one of the hardest things she'd ever done.

Over a week had passed since they'd been truly together. She knew all the reasons they had to stay apart. She knew they had to do it to defray suspicion; she knew she had to do it for her own preservation. In the past five weeks she'd been buffeted by crises and change on all sides. She was hanging on by a thread.

But if she had to wait any longer to see Roberto, she was going to die.

Frannie blinked. A faint pulse of alarm shivered through her. How had this happened? How had she come to need him so much? How, when she'd done her best to keep him at a distance? She'd let him sneak under her guard, she'd let him become a part of her life. She was dependent yet again. And what in God's name was she going to do now?

In time with that thought, she heard his knock and suddenly it all ceased to matter. One moment she was opening the door. The next, she was in Roberto's arms, crushed against him, his mouth sealed to hers. His hands roved over her body, taking ownership, making her shiver. She gloried in the reality of being able to touch him at last.

Roberto made an impatient noise and swung her up in his arms. He carried her down the hall to the room they'd been in two weeks before, this time not to fix the door, but to lay her down on that bed he'd fantasized about.

And do all the things he'd fantasized about next.

She sat up, her legs dangling over the edge. Her fingers raced down the buttons of his shirt and unbuckled his belt. "Now," she said, freeing him.

And stepping up close to the high bed, flipping up her little skirt, he obeyed.

It was hard and deep, fast and furious. There was no patience for undressing, no time for finesse, only an urgent need to come together. He felt her wrap her legs around his waist. He heard her cry out with every surge. He drove them both, recklessly, heedlessly, into that carnal haze where only pleasure had meaning. Control was precarious; the edge was too close.

And then they were there. He felt her tense, saw her throw her head back, heard her cries crescendo. Then she was quaking about him even as she dragged him past the point of no return.

And he knew as they lay after, hearts still racing together, that there was no point of return from her.

Chapter Twelve

Frannie pulled a floral box of photographs out of a cabinet and put it on the kitchen table where she and Roberto were sitting.

"I haven't even gotten them into an album yet," she said apologetically. "There's been a lot going on."

"You don't say," Roberto drawled.

"Anyway, here they are." She spilled them out onto the table. "What did you find out at Lyndsey's?"

"A whole lot and nothing at all," he said.

"What does that mean?"

"She knows something. She didn't want to let me in at first, until I mentioned Josh. I asked her about the Spring Fling and she couldn't keep her stories straight."

"What do you mean?"

"She swears he couldn't possibly have done it, but then she got all upset when I asked her about the fight with Lloyd, which she also swears she didn't know anything about. She said she was with Josh all the time, except later she said she left early, but the time she gave me was after the fight. When I pointed that out, she told me to leave. I think she was there." Roberto locked eyes with her. "And she had his hoodie."

"She's always wearing his shirts and things. Anyway, what's the importance of the hoodie?"

"I thought I told you about this. The guy I saw throw away the crowbar was wearing some kind of black hoodie, just like the one I saw today."

"What?" She stared at him. "You're sure?"

"Positive."

Relief made her lightheaded. "But Josh wasn't wearing a hoodie at the Spring Fling. Look, I'll show you." She shifted through the pictures, hands shaking with barely suppressed excitement. "He was wearing a blue snap-button shirt and his black cowboy hat."

"He could've changed, Frannie."

"When? Before the murder or after? If you saw him running off in a hoodie, he would have to have left his hat somewhere once he put the sweatshirt on. I can tell you for a fact that he didn't have it. Here," she said triumphantly, sliding a photograph across to him. "See? Western shirt and Stetson. Not a hoodie in sight. It wasn't him."

"This doesn't prove anything. He could have put his hat anywhere. He could have put the hoodie on before he met Lloyd to be less obvious, then run off in it, ditched it and come back. Anyway, where's his hat now? Have you seen it since the Spring Fling?"

"Of course," she responded. "It's here. He wore his ball cap to the game tonight."

She took the stairs two at a time to Josh's bedroom, then stopped short at the sight of one of his gray hoodies thrown over the back of his desk chair. It didn't matter, she reminded herself. It wasn't possible that he'd murdered Lloyd, let alone murdered him and brought the blood-soaked clothing home. Roberto was imagining things.

She stepped back into the kitchen to find him still studying the photograph.

"Here it is." She dropped the hat on the table triumphantly.

Roberto didn't look up from the picture.

"Hello? Earth to Roberto."

His eyes flicked from her to the hat, then back to the photograph. A muscle jumped in his jaw.

"Admit it, we were wrong. It's not Josh."

"It's not Josh." He slapped the photo down on the table. "It's me."

For an instant, the words simply refused to register. When they did, it snatched her breath away. Roberto, the killer? "That's not possible," she whispered. "You couldn't have murdered Lloyd. You couldn't have."

Roberto shook his head. "I don't mean the murder. I mean this." He held up the photograph. "This isn't Josh. It's a picture of me."

Relief made her weak, then angry. "Funny," she said shortly, reaching out for the photo.

"No," he said. "I'm serious. Look at it."

It was one of the many crowd shots she'd taken that night, showing people milling about not far from the carnival. Josh was in profile, his hat pulled down low, collar high, the gaudy wash of color from the rides turning his skin rainbow. "I am looking at it. It's Josh. I know my son."

But as the seconds passed, she wasn't so sure. Did the hair look darker, or was it simply the lighting?

"Look at the hat, Frannie," Roberto said softly. "Look at the hatband."

Silver medallions, shining in the lights. But the hat she'd brought downstairs from Josh's room had a band of tiny cobalt-blue beads, a birthday gift to Josh from Lyndsey the year before.

"The band in that picture is made of hand-tooled conchas from a Navajo reservation." Roberto reached over to the chair next to him and lifted up his black Stetson. The silver medallions gleamed. "I bought it about fifteen years ago out in Arizona from the guy who made it. It's one of a kind."

Frannie stared at the photo. And as though it were a game of hidden pictures, she saw what she'd missed— the stronger nose, the shorter hair the broader shoulders. It was Josh, and yet not him. An older brother, maybe, or— And for an instant she felt the room tilt around her. "I must…I must be tired," she said aloud.

There was a buzzing in her ears. The profile in the photo looked like Josh, the way he held his shoulders looked like Josh. She glanced up at the framed picture of him on the étagère opposite the table. And suddenly it was like dominoes falling. "You stand the same way," she said slowly. "Your eyes are set the same. You walk the same way, you— No," she broke off, shaking her head. "No, that's—"

"What? Ridiculous? Is it so far off?"

She shot to her feet, raking her hair back off her face

with both hands. "It's late and I'm getting punchy. We both are. There is no way that—"

"What?"

She shook her head. "It's impossible."

"What? Say it," he demanded, striding over to her.

"It can't be."

"Say it." He caught at her shoulders, forcing her to face him. "Say it. Josh is my son."

"No."

"He's my son, Frannie. He's ours."

"No," she cried out, slapping at his chest, and then her hands turned to fists and she was pummeling him, "No, no, no," she repeated, tears sliding crazily down her cheeks, her voice half-hysterical.

He folded his arms around her, trapping her against him until she quieted.

"My whole life…" she whispered brokenly against his chest.

And in that moment, looking down at her stricken face he understood Lloyd's assailant because for the first time in his life, he truly wanted to hurt someone.

And if Cindy Fortune had been there in that moment, he wouldn't have been responsible for what he would have done.

"Sit." He folded Frannie into a chair and one after another, yanked open the cabinet doors. "Do you have any liquor? Whiskey?" He found the bottles and poured them both a couple of fingers of tequila. He thumped Frannie's tumbler down before her. "Here, drink."

"I don't—"

"Drink it," he ordered.

He knocked back his own shot, but it didn't do much

to calm him. Instead, he paced. "You and I had sex the night after you were with Lloyd."

"But the results of the DNA test—"

"I don't give a damn about the DNA test. It's true. You and I both know it. And I have a pretty good idea who did it."

"My...mother?"

"Who else would have had reason? Not Lloyd's family, not you. It had to be her."

"But how?" Frannie stood. "It's a lab test. She couldn't just magically change it."

"She wanted me out of your life and she wanted Lloyd in. And she was ready to do whatever it took, including recruiting help."

"So everything I've lived through in the last nineteen years is because of a lie?" Frannie's voice rose. "Because of *her?*" She snatched up a porcelain figurine from the étagère, whirling to fling it against the wall. It burst into fragments.

"Hey, easy."

"Don't tell me easy," she rounded on him. "She lied to me. She gave me to Lloyd like I was chattel." She flung her hands up. "My *God.*"

Roberto welcomed the bright flare of anger, something to take away that terrifying fragility. He watched as she strode back and forth.

"This is crazy. Half of me can't understand how I could have missed it. The other half says there's no way it could be true or I would have figured it out years ago. Josh was blond when he was younger, explain that," she challenged.

"So are you. So was my grandmother. Why are you

fighting this? Do you not want to believe it because you can't accept that your mother did this to you? Or because you don't want him to be mine?"

"I don't want to believe it because I can't accept that half my life has been built on a lie."

"And mine, too." He caught at her hands. "But Josh is real. I'm real. What you and I feel for each other is real. The lies that kept us apart are in the past now. What matters is right here."

"It's not that easy, Roberto."

"Easy? You think this is easy?" he asked, spinning away in frustration. "I don't even have words for how I feel right now. We've been robbed, Frannie, all of us, years taken away, just stolen. And if I think about it too long I'm going to lose it." He strode back and forth, eyes on her. "So I'd rather focus on what I can change, and what I can do and what comes next. You tell me, what do we do now?"

She stared at him. "What do we do now?"

"There's Josh. What do we say to him? How do we get the test redone? How do we deal with Cindy?"

Even the thought of her mother generated a wave of fury so powerful it made Frannie feel vaguely sick. "I can't handle dealing with her right now."

"Josh, then. What do we tell him? How do we confirm the results? How do we become a family?"

"A family?" What she'd always longed for and yet it seemed like an illusion, something to be snatched away the instant she began to believe in it. Happiness wasn't a part of her life. Reality had never been so kind.

But Roberto believed in it. "He's our son. We belong together, we always have. Cindy did her best to keep us apart, but it didn't work. And maybe it's late, but there's still time."

Cindy. Her stomach roiled. "You're going too fast," Frannie said sharply. "Stop." There were too many changes all at once, too many emotions buffeting her. Jet fighters trying to turn too quickly broke apart under the strain, she thought, the way she felt like things were breaking apart. Everything she'd experienced for nineteen years was a lie, every nightmare moment she'd endured had occurred in a prison of her mother's making. She'd nearly been destroyed, and now to discover that it should never have happened made her almost dizzy.

"I love you, Frannie," Roberto said. "I want us to be together. Didn't you tell me how you used to imagine that Josh was mine? Now it's real. We can make it real."

"It's too fast," she said again, circling around the table. "You don't understand. My entire life has been turned upside down. Lloyd wasn't just verbally abusive, Roberto. He hit me. Not often, but he made it count when he did."

"That bas—"

"But I survived it," she cut him off. "I survived it, and I lived through it day after day because I told myself that Josh needed his father, however poor a specimen he was. I told myself that it was a bed of my own making, that I'd made my choice long ago and that if anybody had to suffer for it, it would be me.

"And now you're telling me that it wasn't so at all? I can't just shrug it off, don't you see? I can't just say okay, good on me, and march ahead without a thought," she said, the words tumbling out. "You want to make up for lost time? I'm just trying to keep up. Five weeks ago, Lloyd was murdered. Three weeks ago, I was still in jail." She pressed her fingertips against her eyelids. "It's been one thing after another and it just keeps coming. I care about you, Roberto, I truly do, but I feel like I'm in a cement mixer that just keeps turning. I've got to find some way to make it stop before I can figure out what to do next. The only thing that hasn't been taken from me in the last five weeks is my son."

"Our son, who's been kept from me for eighteen years. Don't you understand, Frannie? It's time to set everything right. I love you and I want us all to be a family together, the way we were supposed to be."

"That's what Mom said about Lloyd…"

He slammed his fist down on the table. "Goddammit, I am not Lloyd Fredericks."

"But you're pushing me to do what you want me to do regardless of whether I'm ready or not," she flung at him. "Is that how life would be with you after the sweet talk went away, Roberto? Everything by your rules, everything on your schedule? I keep telling you I need more time, and *you don't listen.*"

"I want to be there for you," he exploded. "With you. Josh is my son. We should have been married years ago. We should be married now."

"This isn't a square dance. I don't just belong to whoever Josh's father happens to be this week. We aren't a package deal."

"Is that what you think this is about?" Roberto demanded. "Dammit, Frannie, it's not just about Josh, it's you. I love you. I always have. I never stopped, not once. Even when I thought you had sent me away."

He linked his fingers together on top of his head and looked at the ceiling. "Frannie, you're not the only one who got robbed. I got robbed, too. We all did. Josh was robbed by not knowing who he was his entire life, by having to deal with a man like Lloyd Fredericks. I was robbed of watching my son grow. You and I were robbed of a life together. And I'm really angry and want to make it right. I want to get something redeemable out of it— we all deserve that. And the only way I can think that can happen is doing what we both want—to be together."

"I couldn't do that right now even if I wanted to, Roberto," she blazed. "And I don't want to, not while you're pushing."

"I'm pushing because we've already lost too much time. We've already waited too long."

"You won't wait? You want an answer now? It's no, okay?"

"You don't mean that. You know it's right with us, you know it. You can't walk away from this."

"Are you forgetting why we decided to stay apart in the first place? The murder, the police? There's too much going on with that and Cindy's accident, and the notes and the fires and—"

The notes...

One of the Fortunes is not who you think.

"Oh my God," she started. "'One of the Fortunes—'"

"'—is not who you think.' Josh," Roberto added grimly.

"They know. Whoever's behind the notes and the fires and all of it, they *know*. It's all connected." She turned for the wall phone. "We've got to call Ross. Cindy has to have some idea about this, she has to."

"What we've got to do is go to the cops."

"Are you out of your mind?" Frannie asked. "Go to the police? Tell them all of this?"

"Frannie, we have to. It's gone past us, now, don't you understand? Don't you remember that note after the second fire, 'This one wasn't an accident, either'? Someone set those fires and maybe that same person cut Cindy's brake lines. She could've been killed. If this keeps going, someone will be, someone—" He stopped.

"Lloyd." Frannie's voice was barely audible.

They locked eyes with each other, the ticking of the clock very loud in the silence.

"We've got to find out what really happened at the Spring Fling," Roberto said. "We've got to find out what Josh knows."

"He doesn't know anything," she shot back. "He wasn't your hoodie-wearing murderer."

Roberto caught her arms in his hands. "Even if he's not, we still need to know what he knows. We can't just keep dancing around this. It's got to end, Frannie. We've got to talk to Josh."

"Talk to Josh about what?" a voice asked.

And heart pounding, Frannie turned to see her son standing at the door that led in from the garage.

Chapter Thirteen

Frannie swallowed. "Oh. Honey, hi." She turned to sit on one of the chairs at the breakfast bar. "How was the baseball game?"

"Fine." Josh gave Roberto a hard look, shutting the garage door. "What's going on? What did you want to talk to me about?"

"What happened at the Spring Fling."

"Roberto, this isn't the time," Frannie cut in, an edge in her voice.

He shook his head. "We can't just keep pretending there isn't a problem, not anymore. You spent two weeks in jail because you were afraid to mention it." He turned to Josh. "We need to know whatever you can tell us about your…father at the Spring Fling."

Josh glanced down. "What do you mean?"

"You had an argument with him."

He shrugged. "So we fought. We always fought. It was no big deal." He walked to the refrigerator and got out a soft drink.

"It didn't sound that way to the people who heard you."

"Who heard?" he asked a little too quickly.

"I did," Frannie said. "You were right behind the tent I was working in."

Roberto watched Josh take a seat at the table, stretching out his legs, trying a little too hard to look at ease. The kid—his kid, he thought with inward amazement—concentrated on his Mountain Dew. An attempt to avoid eye contact or garden-variety teenager?

Josh took a swallow of his drink. "Why the third degree all of a sudden?"

"We just want your help, Josh," Frannie told him. "We need to find the killer."

"It sounds like Sherlock Holmes here thinks I'm the killer."

Roberto walked closer. "I'm just trying to get information. Right now, your mother's still the only one charged for the murder. That means until they catch the person who did it, she's still at risk."

Josh's faux relaxation vanished. "They can't bring her back in, can they?"

"Yes, actually, they can. There's a big difference between being released on her own recognizance and having the charges dropped," Roberto commented. "Maybe now you understand why I'm asking questions. And sooner or later, the cops are going to be asking questions about you because someone's going to tell them about your fight. Not your mom, but other people.

You were too close to the tents, too loud." Roberto watched him closely. "And you threatened him."

"It wasn't any big deal. It was just trash talk."

"Lyndsey got upset when I asked her about it."

He gave Roberto a sharp look. "You had no right to go over and grill her."

Interesting that that was what provoked a reaction. "She told you, then. I thought she might."

"Leave her alone. You got questions, ask me."

"Gladly. Do you know anything about your father's murder?"

"No." The answer came out almost before Roberto finished the question.

"Does Lyndsey?"

He glanced away. "No."

"What does she know, Josh?"

"Nothing." Pulling off his ball cap, he scraped his hair back. He wasn't sprawled out now, but hunched over the table tensely.

"She's hiding something. It's pretty clear."

"Forget about Lyndsey, already, will you? She didn't do anything."

And suddenly all the vague disquiet coalesced and Roberto knew. "It was her, wasn't it?"

"What?"

"You didn't kill Lloyd Fredericks. It was Lyndsey."

Josh shot to his feet. "That's nuts," he said angrily.

"It's also true."

"Josh?" Frannie stood. "Is it?"

His eyes skated to one side. "No way. She had nothing to do with it."

"She was there for the fight, wasn't she?" Roberto probed.

"I'm not saying anything." Josh crossed his arms stubbornly, jaw set exactly like Jorge's did when he was in trouble.

"Stop taking care of her."

"I can't," he flared. "You of all people should get that. You protect the people you care about."

"Yeah? Then how about protecting your mother and stopping lying for the person who killed your father?" Roberto snapped.

The words hung in the air. The minutes stretched out in a humming silence. Roberto held his breath.

"It was an accident." Josh's voice was barely audible. He looked from the tabletop to Frannie. "She only told me tonight. I swear I didn't know when you were locked up, Mom. She's been a little weird lately, moody sometimes, but I figured it was just..."

"What?"

Josh stared up at the ceiling and blew out a breath. "She's pregnant," he said flatly, staring from one to the other.

"Pregnant?" Frannie croaked.

"We tried to be careful. She was supposed to be on the pill, it's just, you know...stuff happens."

"Why didn't you say something?"

"Say something?" An edge entered his voice. "After you and Dad spent the whole last year trying to get me to break up with her? If I'd told you she was pregnant, all you would have done was say I told you so."

"No, I wouldn't have," Frannie said vehemently. "My God, don't you think I know what it's like? I've been there, Josh. I know how scary and overwhelming it feels. I just wish you'd told me so you didn't have to go through it alone."

"I wasn't alone." Josh raised his chin. "I had Lyndsey. We were together."

We were together.

Roberto felt like he'd been punched in the stomach. He hadn't been able to be there for Frannie all those years ago. They hadn't been together. The reason why didn't matter; the fact was that she'd endured it without him.

The first of only many things.

He shook his mind loose from the thought. "What happened at the Spring Fling, Josh?"

Josh sighed. "I was taking that vase out to your car, Mom, like you asked. Lyndsey was with me. We were talking about the baby, and all of a sudden Dad was there. He went ballistic, yelling and saying stuff about Lyndsey—really bad stuff—and I don't know, I just kind of lost it myself." Defiance flashed in his eyes.

"I know," Frannie said gently. "I've never heard you sound like that before."

"I didn't want him around Lyndsey—he was acting crazy—so I put the vase in her hands and told her to leave and meet me at the dance. But I guess she got worried and came back...." He raised his hands helplessly.

"Anyway, I finally told Dad to go to hell and walked away, but Lyndsey was still back there. She said the vase was too heavy. She put it down under a tarp where it would be safe, but she saw Dad coming toward her and she got scared. There was this crowbar sticking out from under the tarp, and...she grabbed it.

"All she wanted to do was walk past him, get back

to where people were, but he wouldn't leave her alone." A muscle jumped in Josh's jaw. "He was talking all kinds of trash about how he knew girls like her, girls who trapped guys, girls who spread their legs for money, just evil stuff, Mom, evil."

But it hadn't been Lyndsey Lloyd had been talking to that night, Frannie understood. She closed her eyes a moment. "What happened then?"

"He said he wasn't going to let her trap me with the baby, so he grabbed her and put his hands around her neck and started to strangle her." Josh looked at them both, misery in his eyes. "She hit him with the bar because she had to, Mom, she had to. He was going to kill her. She was blacking out. And when she woke up, he was dead and there was blood all over. So she ran away." He put his head in his hands. Frannie walked over and put her arms around his shoulders.

"If she and Lloyd fought, why didn't anyone hear?" Roberto asked.

"Are you trying to say she's lying?" Josh raised his head to glare at him. "She's telling the truth. He tried to kill her. And now she's scared to death that they'll find out and she'll go to jail."

Roberto folded his arms. "Your mom can tell her what it's like."

"Roberto." Frannie shot him a look of warning, then turned to Josh. "Honey, if it happened the way she said, there's no jury in the world that would convict her. It would be self-defense."

"Are you telling me to call the cops on her?" he asked incredulously. "I can't turn her in. She's going to have my kid. And I…I love her."

"Nobody's talking about calling the cops." Roberto took a seat. "The best thing for her to do is turn herself in."

Josh shook his head. "No way. She's never going to do that. She's too scared."

"What about if we go talk to her?" Frannie said. "The three of us. We'll convince her and then we'll go to the police together."

"She won't listen."

Roberto rested his elbows on the table. "She's got to, Josh, or else we have to call the cops. Unless you want to chance your mom going to trial for a murder she didn't commit. We need to talk to Lyndsey. Now."

"Tomorrow," Frannie corrected. "It's after midnight. It's too late."

"The sooner she turns herself in, the better it's going to be for her," Roberto countered. "And as long as we know and don't act, we're accessories. Her mother works the night shift, we can catch her alone. Let's just go do it."

"She's going to hate me for telling," Josh said miserably.

Frannie touched his cheek. "You're trying to help her, honey. Eventually, she'll see that. Sometimes you have to make difficult choices in life. That's what you do for people you care about."

The minutes stretched out. Josh sat in silence, staring at his hands. Finally, he raised his head. "Being an adult sucks."

"It has its moments," Roberto agreed. "So what do you say?"

Josh nodded. "Okay." He swallowed. "Let's roll."

The yellow bug light at Lyndsey's house cast a faint amber glow over the uneven boards of the porch. Josh had given Lyndsey a call on the way over. Now, he gave Frannie and Roberto a sickly smile and knocked on the door.

It opened immediately. "Come in, quick," Lyndsey demanded, "or old lady Quinson across the street will—" She stopped, staring at Frannie and Roberto. "What are they doing here?"

There was none of the indecision of earlier that day, Roberto noticed. The look in her eyes was downright hostile. And she wore the black hoodie.

"Let us in, Lyns," Josh said. "We need to talk to you."

"My mom's going to be really mad if she gets wind of this. I'm not supposed to have people over when she's working."

"I'll talk to her," Frannie promised. "We'll only be here for a few minutes."

She'd been watching television, Roberto saw as they walked into the living room, *Romeo and Juliet* reset in what looked like modern-day Miami. An open soda sat on the coffee table by the couch. In what looked to be long-standing habit, Lyndsey and Josh sat next to each other. Frannie chose the remaining chair; Roberto just leaned against the wall by the entryway.

Lyndsey muted the television. "Why are you back here?" she asked Roberto.

"Same thing as this morning—the murder of Lloyd Fredericks," Roberto said.

"And like I said to you this morning, I don't know anything about it."

"It's okay, Lyns," Josh said gently. "I told them."

She blinked. "Told them? You told them what?"

"What happened between you and Dad."

For a moment her expression turned absolutely livid, then it relaxed, so quickly Roberto couldn't be sure he'd seen it. "Nothing happened with me and your dad."

"Lyndsey, it was self-defense," Frannie said gently. "If you turn yourself in to the police, that's what they'll say. You won't have to go to jail."

"Of course I won't. I didn't do anything."

"It's not that easy. They have forensic evidence," Roberto gambled. "Your blood on the vase, your fingerprints on the murder weapon. The best thing you can do is turn yourself in. It'll work in your favor, especially if the self-defense angle holds up."

"Of course it will hold up." Josh's voice held equal parts anger and protectiveness. "You didn't see my dad that night. He lost it completely. She's lucky she's alive."

At that, Lyndsey's eyes filled with tears. "I didn't mean to. I thought he was going to kill me."

Josh slipped his arms around her. "It's going to be okay."

"I'm afraid," she whispered. "What if they put me in jail?"

"They won't."

"Lyndsey, you can't live with this hanging over your head forever," Frannie said. "You have to confess. It's for the best. There will be a trial, but we'll all testify for you."

Lyndsey chewed on her lip. "Do I have to decide now?"

"The sooner you do it, the better," Roberto said. "We all know now, Lyndsey, and there's no way we can cover it up. Just turn yourself in. Everything will be fine."

Lyndsey swallowed. "All right," she whispered. "Just let me go call my mom and tell her."

She walked past Roberto and through the swinging

door that led to the kitchen. And he could hear her let loose the tears she'd been holding back. They all could.

Josh stared down at his hands, looking sick. "I did this. It's my fault."

"You didn't do anything." Roberto wanted to squeeze the kid's shoulder, do something, but it wasn't his place. Yet.

Instead, Frannie rose to go sit by him. "Sometimes things just happen." Her voice was soft, reassuring. "It's going to be okay, you'll see. It'll all work out."

"You bet it will," There was a click and they all turned to see Lyndsey standing at the kitchen door, a gun in her hand.

Chapter Fourteen

For a frozen instant, no one moved. *A gun,* Frannie thought numbly. A quick squeeze of the trigger and any one of them would be gone instantly.

Josh blinked as though he couldn't make sense of what he was seeing. "Lyns, what are you doing?"

"Move away from her, Josh," Lyndsey ordered.

Frannie felt the quick rush of adrenaline. Not her son, she vowed, the numbness gone. If she had to physically throw herself in front of the bullet, she was going to make sure Josh came out of this whole.

"I'm not going anywhere," Josh returned. "This isn't the way. Don't hurt my family."

"It's not like I want to." She strode over to stand opposite them. "They're making me. No way am I going down to the police department and turning myself in."

"Lyndsey, you've got to. It's going to be okay. You'll get off with self-defense."

She laughed. "Is that what they told you? Of course they did," she answered her own question. "What else are they going to say? They want me to take the fall so that your mother gets off. But no way in hell is that ever going to happen."

This matter-of-fact calculation was far more dangerous than fear or anger, Frannie realized.

And maybe Roberto did, too, because he stepped forward a pace. Lyndsey whirled to face him. "Don't move or I'll shoot you right now," she threatened.

"No!" Frannie burst out in horror, starting up from the couch. Time broke into a series of images: flickering actors fighting on the television screen, Roberto standing, tension coiled in him like a spring, Lyndsey's face pale, the gun in her shaking hands.

The gun.

And in that moment of fear, Frannie realized what she'd tried so hard to block.

She was in love with Roberto.

"Lyndsey, you can't do this," she protested. "What about your baby?"

The round circle of the barrel swung toward her. "Shut up," Lyndsey snapped. "I should have killed you, too."

Frannie felt rather than saw Roberto tense. "Don't," she said under her breath. He couldn't put himself at risk, not now that she'd finally understood how much he truly mattered.

And what a desert her life would be without him.

"What are you doing?" Josh demanded.

"Don't distract me, Josh. I'm doing what I have to."

There was something in Lyndsey's eyes, Frannie realized, not panic precisely, but more the wary look of some sharp-toothed creature that hid in its burrow and only came out at night. For the first time, she understood that they weren't dealing with an entirely rational individual.

And her head became oddly clear. "We can work this out." Frannie kept her voice even. "We'll get lawyers. It wasn't your fault."

Say whatever it takes to get out of the room, whatever it takes to survive this so that you can tell him.

But Lyndsey wasn't buying it. "There's no way they'd let me go. Not after everything I've done."

"What's that?" Roberto asked.

She laughed. "Oh, we've been having fun." She took a few restless steps across the living room. "I liked seeing you Fortunes worried. For once, you weren't in control. For once, you were the ones who were scared. Like you're scared now."

"You were the one behind the fires and the notes, weren't you?" Frannie asked.

Lyndsey laughed. "Give the lady an A plus." Her face relaxed into the benign expression of a high-schooler talking about the latest download for her iPod. "I only did it for Josh and me. And for the baby. I'm going to call her Sarah, after my grandmother."

"For the baby?" Roberto brought her back to the subject.

"Of course." Impatient, she paced a few more steps. "Don't look at me like that, Josh. You've got to take the big-picture view. I mean, how could we get married and start a family if your dad and your mom—" she shot

a look of silky dislike at Frannie "—were in the way? I
had to stop that somehow."

"Josh is eighteen. He's gotten his inheritance. What
could his parents have done anyway?"

She looked at Roberto pityingly. "You don't get it, do
you? The Fortunes own this town. We didn't have a
choice. We had to put the screws to Lloyd. We had to
scare him."

"Who's we?"

Roberto was pumping the girl gently, making her
give details, keeping her going each time she stopped.
If they ever got out of the room alive, Frannie thought,
there would be enough to convict her for her crimes.

If they ever got out alive.

"*We* was my mom and me. We had it all planned out."

"It didn't work, though, did it?"

"I thought he'd be smarter," she complained, beginning to cross the room again like an erratic pendulum.
"The fires and the notes were to soften him up, but it
took him a while to get it. And it was so simple. All he
had to do was stop making a fuss about us, and Mom
and I would keep our mouths shut. If he kept it up, we'd
see that he lost everything."

Josh frowned, looking from Lyndsey to Roberto.
"What the hell are you talking about?"

"Lloyd loved being a Fortune." Lyndsey had an
almost dreamy look in her eyes. "See, you guys are born
with it. You don't know what it's like on the outside."

"But you and I do, don't we, Lyndsey?" Roberto said.
Say whatever it takes to get out of the room.

"I guess you would," Lyndsey nodded to herself.
"They say your families are friends, but you Mendozas

get the short end of the stick every time, don't you? Anybody who deals with the Fortunes does. They have everything." Her voice filled with sudden venom as she glared at Frannie.

"But Lloyd was a Fredericks," Roberto reminded her.

Lyndsey gave him a scornful look. "We both know that doesn't count for anything anymore. But being a part of the Fortunes sure does. We had to threaten to take that away so that he'd behave."

"But that would affect Josh, too."

"You think I wanted to do this? I did it because I had to. I did it for us, Josh."

"For us?" Josh repeated. "That's why you burned my aunt's barn down?"

"Of course, silly," she said affectionately, missing his rancor. "Lloyd was in the way. And he was going to try to con money out of you, money that belonged to us and to Sarah. So I told him if he didn't watch out, we were going to tell everybody the truth."

"Tell everybody what?" Josh asked.

She made an impatient noise. "Jeez, Josh, how can you be so dense? He wasn't your real dad."

How do we tell him, Roberto had asked. Frannie had never in a million years imagined this would be the way.

Josh shook his head. "That's nuts."

"How can you be so sure, Lyndsey?" The question was out before Frannie knew she was going to ask it. Josh snapped his head around to stare at her.

"My mom's a nurse. She worked in the clinic that did the testing. Cindy brought money, lots of it. When the test results came in, Mom just switched them. It was easy, she said."

"I don't believe it." Frowning, Josh looked at Frannie. And then he seemed to realize that she wasn't surprised.

"My mom used part of the money to buy this house," Lyndsey continued, making another of her now-regular swings across the room. "Then my dad left. It got harder. I mean, look at this place. It's a dump, now. You Fortunes all live in palaces. And here's Cindy Fortune living the good life while Mom and I are scraping to get by."

For an instant, pure hatred flashed in her eyes. And then, unnervingly quickly, she returned to sunny and serene. "My mom went back a couple years ago and asked her for some more money. Really reasonable, just asking one person to another, can you help?"

Blackmail, Frannie thought. *Really reasonable.*

"You would have thought that Mom was asking her to open a vein. Cindy threatened to tell everybody. She said she'd make sure Mom lost her license if she tried anything. But we got her back good." Lyndsey smiled in satisfaction. "A little snip here, a little snip there."

"You cut Cindy Fortune's brake lines?" Roberto asked.

Lyndsey looked positively beatific. "It was hard not to laugh, seeing her walk around all banged up after her accident. It's too bad it didn't work. That's because you Fortunes always wind up on top. But not this time. It was fun to see you all afraid. You didn't feel so important then, did you?"

"You're talking about my family," Josh ground out.

"Oh, honey, I don't mean you. I love you. I can't wait to marry you and get our own place and raise our baby together. Lots of babies," she said smiling. "With your inheritance, we'll be able to afford them.

"That's all I ever wanted," she explained. "But Lloyd

tried to mess everything up. Lloyd and you." Her mouth twisted as she stopped pacing and pointed the gun at Frannie. "You're why we had to go after Lloyd. It's your fault I had to be at the Spring Fling, telling him how it was going to go. I was going to fill you in as insurance," she added to Roberto, "but Lloyd sort of changed my plans."

"You were the one who called about the meet."

"Fooled you, huh?"

"Not really. The phone booth you called from was in this neighborhood, I looked up the number. What did Lloyd say after you told him his choices? Is that why you hit him?"

"He deserved it." She paced faster, agitated. "He said I was lying, he called me all kinds of names. And then he knocked me over and I hit my nose on your danged vase." She threw Frannie a malevolent look. "I thought I broke it. It bled like a stuck pig. But I showed him. It's like my daddy always said, 'you knock me down you'd better kill me because I'll make you sorry.' He never even heard me coming," she added with relish. "I whapped him a good one."

Frannie felt a chill.

"With the bar?" Roberto shifted his weight a bit. "That must have been hard. He was a lot taller than you. And stronger."

"I got him from behind as he was walking away. There was so much blood," Lyndsey said wonderingly, looking down so that she missed Roberto sliding one foot back to brace himself. "I didn't think I hit him that hard. It hurt my hand." She rubbed it against her jeans absently. "I had blood all over me, but I put on Josh's hoodie and threw away the crowbar. I got a ride into town with a trucker."

"It wasn't self-defense at all," Frannie said. "It was murder."

"You think I wanted to do that? He made me," Lyndsey snarled.

"Of course he did," Roberto said. "I know how it is, having people tell you you're not good enough for their family. It wasn't your fault. You were only doing what you had to." He eyed the arc of Lyndsey's steps, calculating. "They don't understand what it does to you to know that's what they think, every day, every night, every time you look in the mirror. And what it's like to not have enough. You and I, we know what that's like, Lyndsey."

"Yes," she whispered, walking closer.

"It eats at you. And to be pulled into Cindy Fortune's schemes and hardly get anything out of it?" He flicked a glance back at Frannie. "I'd have done just what you did. I would have been so mad. And that kind of mad makes you want to hurt someone, doesn't it?"

"Yes."

"Lots of people get mad," Frannie interrupted, praying she'd read Roberto's look right. "You don't see them murdering people."

"You bitch!" Eyes narrowed with fury, Lyndsey pivoted toward Frannie, bringing the gun up. And in that moment, Roberto sprang at her.

Noise and confusion, the tangle of limbs. Lyndsey fought Roberto for the gun with the adrenaline-soaked strength of the unbalanced. They rolled and wrestled on the floor as she screamed in fury, as Josh leapt over the coffee table to try to help pin the girl.

Frannie snatched up the telephone receiver on the side table.

"Nine-one-one operator, can I help you?"

There was the roar of a gunshot, the muzzle flash, the scent of cordite. And a choking fear as Frannie looked to see blood spreading on the rug.

"Come quickly," she whispered. "Someone's been shot."

Roberto punched the button on the vending machine, watching the cup fall down and the stream of coffee begin. There was something about hospitals that seemed to exist outside of time. It seemed that he had always been here, waiting for word, that it was endless, like those nightmare moments in Lyndsey's living room when she'd pointed the gun at Frannie and he'd felt his heart stop in fear.

"I thought I might find you here."

Roberto turned to see Len Wheeler. He turned back. "Where's your sidekick?"

"Writing up the initial reports. Don't worry about him."

"Wheeler, right now I can't say I give a damn about either of you." Roberto opened the little window and pulled out his coffee.

"I guess you have a right to feel like that."

Roberto's brows lowered. "Is that the best you can do? You lock Frannie up for two weeks, you sweat me down, the only way you find out anything is when we deliver it to you and all you can say is I have a right to feel like that?"

"I won't apologize for being skeptical because that's the nature of our business, but I saw the hoodie. You were telling the truth."

"For all the good it did me."

"For everybody who tells us the truth, there are twice as many lying."

"Isn't it your job to be able to tell the difference?"

"Yeah, the day I get to be perfect at it, I'll let you know." Wheeler fished in his pocket for change and stepped over to the machine.

"How about you skip that and just tell me what the hell is going on? I saw you hauling somebody out in handcuffs when we were in the E.R."

"Donna Pollack. Lyndsey's mother. McCaskill questioned her." Wheeler smiled faintly. "She takes a dim view of the Fortunes."

"Not nearly as dim a view as the Fortunes take of her. How's the daughter? Josh will want to know."

The coins jingled as Wheeler fed them into the slot. "I talked to the doc. They're still closing up, but he said the surgery to remove the bullet is done. Her leg should heal up with no problem."

"And the baby?"

"They think it's going to be fine."

"Tell Josh."

"Already did. Stopped in to see him and Miz Fredericks just before I came to find you. He still wants to stay until the girl's out. Not that the staff is allowed to tell him anything because of privacy laws."

"But you're going to keep him posted, aren't you, Wheeler?" Roberto asked with an edge to his voice. "Don't forget, we handed this case to you gift-wrapped."

Wheeler pulled his coffee out of the machine and walked to the little ledge that held sugar and creamer. "We had to wake up a judge to sign the search warrant, but McCaskill went through the Pollacks' garage. Found the same accelerants used for the arson fires and a pair of clippers with what looks like brake fluid on them. 'Pears that everything Lyndsey Pollack told you is true, maybe down to Josh Fredericks' parentage. Hell of a thing." He shook his head. "Hell of a thing."

"Yeah. Enjoy your coffee." Roberto turned for the door. Time to get back up to the O.R. waiting room and back to Frannie.

"Hey, Mendoza," Wheeler said. When Roberto glanced back, he gave him a level look. "I'm sorry everything worked out so crappy."

"You and me both."

Hell of a thing, Roberto thought as he rode the elevator to the surgical unit. The words weren't adequate to the occasion, but then again, he couldn't think of any that were. It seemed unimaginably long ago that he and Frannie had discovered Cindy's initial machinations to keep them apart. The shock of that seemed like nothing compared to what this day had brought.

If he let himself stop and think, he'd be reeling over it, and he was an adult. What was it like for a kid like Josh to discover that everything he believed about himself was a lie? Eighteen wasn't old enough to deal with that; hell, thirty-nine wasn't.

Roberto stepped out of the elevator car and turned toward the little waiting area at the end of the hall where windows looked out at a landscape now coming gradually into view with the approach of the day.

Josh sat in one of the chairs before the window, bent over his thighs, staring at his hands dangling between his knees. Next to him, Frannie leaned in to smooth back his hair and murmur something. Everything about her posture spoke of exhaustion, and yet still she found the strength to reassure, to support.

I feel like I'm in a cement mixer that just keeps turning, she'd told Roberto in a conversation that seemed like it had taken place a million years before. But right now, she wasn't paying attention to her own turmoil. She was focusing on taking care of her son. Their son. It was something he should have been a part of, Roberto thought in frustration, something they should have done together.

As he moved to go to her, Josh suddenly turned to lean his head into Frannie's shoulder. She slipped her arms around him in a gesture of such tenderness that it brought an ache to Roberto's throat.

And suddenly, he understood what she'd been trying to tell him all along. It didn't matter about him. Maybe it didn't even matter about them. What mattered was her taking care of Josh.

Give me time and space to deal with everything, she'd begged, but Roberto hadn't listened. He'd wanted, needed to make something happen between the two of them, to change what had gone before. But that wasn't important right now.

Despite how shattered she had to be, right now Frannie's only thoughts were of their son. That was the thing he'd missed, that loving someone meant putting aside your own wants to give them what they needed— even if what you wanted was to take care of them. In some alternative universe, he and Frannie and Josh might have been the perfect family. In this one, Roberto had to accept that here was maybe something he couldn't help. His steps slowed to a stop. Maybe here was something he finally needed to let go.

In the window behind where Frannie and Josh sat, he could just glimpse the first rays of the rising sun. Frannie turned to look out at the rose-stained horizon, and the light turned her hair into a glowing nimbus.

And as he had done on a dawn nineteen years before, Roberto Mendoza turned away and started walking.

Chapter Fifteen

"All rise." The bailiff stood at the front of the court-room. "Court is now in session, the Honorable Justice Constance Hamel presiding."

The Red Rock County Courthouse had been built in the 1920s, with the soaring ceilings and marble floors of the days before air-conditioning. There was a grandeur to the oaken paneling and bronze light fixtures, the burgundy velvet drapes that bracketed the tall win-dows. Over the course of the trial, Frannie had come to know them all well.

It seemed like a lifetime since that frozen tableau in Lyndsey's living room, but in reality only three months had passed, half of that spent waiting for Lyndsey to heal. By the standards of a city like Los Angeles or New York, perhaps, to go from crime to sentencing in the remaining six weeks was blindingly quick. To

Frannie, it felt like forever that her life had been bounded by these four walls, bracketed by the morning announcements of the bailiff and the smack of the gavel at the end of the day.

It felt like forever since Roberto had been gone from her life.

"In case number eight-oh-eight, the State of Texas versus Pollack, Lyndsey, we are ready for sentencing," announced Judge Hamel, a brisk, no-nonsense woman who'd nonetheless shown surprising compassion in dealing with both Josh and Lyndsey. "We've already heard opening statements and character evidence. Prosecution, would you like to make your closing statement?"

"We would, Your Honor."

Had Frannie once told Roberto that her life made her feel like she was in a cement mixer? It didn't, it felt more like being trapped in an avalanche, taking blow after blow while never knowing precisely where she was. There had been a moment of the gunshot, followed by the blind gratitude of knowing that both Josh and Roberto were safe. And then the police and the EMTs had descended.

And somewhere during the endless hours in the hospital, Roberto had slipped away. He sat now, farther down the row from her in a blue suit and burgundy tie, looking heartbreakingly handsome. And all it did was hurt.

"Would the defense like to make a closing statement?" Judge Hamel asked.

"Yes, Your Honor." The public defender, a pretty brunette in a sober gray suit, rose to her feet.

Frannie had heard through the grapevine that Roberto

was back in Denver. Oh, sure, he'd shown up for court dates, but he'd always managed to keep his distance and always managed to slip away without speaking to her. As the weeks had gone by, it had become increasingly difficult for her to convince herself it was anything but intentional.

She supposed she could have picked up the phone and called him. If she'd been a different kind of person, perhaps she would've flown to Denver. But she'd done neither.

Maybe he blamed her for what Cindy had done. Maybe Frannie had driven him off with what she'd said the night they discovered the truth about Josh. Maybe he'd just decided it was all too much. Or maybe he'd simply lost interest. He'd always been a man who knew what he wanted, and maybe, after the excitement of the reunion had faded, what he wanted was no longer her.

What was hardest was that she'd never had a chance to tell him how she felt. And now sentencing was here, perhaps the last day that she would see him. Even though they shared a son, Josh was an adult and perfectly capable of pursuing his own relationship with his father.

And so she sat and concentrated on the closing statements and tried not to let the misery well up.

Judge Hamel cleared her throat. "In the case of the state versus Pollack, Lyndsey, we are ready to pronounce sentence. Will the defendant please stand?"

In the end, it came out perhaps better than they could've anticipated. Donna Pollack was sentenced to a total of sixteen years in prison and thirty-thousand dollars in fines for her counts of arson, and attempted murder in the case of Cindy Fortune's car accident. For

Lyndsey, though, there would be no prison. Instead, she would see the inside of a psychiatric hospital, and Josh and Frannie would have custody of the child after it was born.

Frannie sighed, rising. It was done.

She didn't think she could bear it.

She rose and began to walk toward the aisle then stopped. Roberto stood there, his eyes steady on hers. "Frannie, how are you?"

It hurt to even look at him. "I'm fine, how are you?"

"Better now, I think. How's it going, Josh? You okay with the verdicts?"

Josh shrugged. "Yeah, I guess so."

They waited for long minutes in silence as the courtroom emptied out. There had been a time they'd talked for hours. How was it possible that now she could think of nothing except the words she couldn't say?

Roberto glanced down at her as they started to move up the aisle to the door. "Are you going to need help with the reporters?" he asked.

"We're parked out back. We should be fine."

"I guess you've gotten good at avoiding the media circus."

She let Josh walk a little way ahead of her. "We've learned a few tricks. None as good as leaving town, but they work."

There was a beat of silence. "I guess maybe I deserve that," Roberto said quietly.

Frannie shook her head. "I'm sorry. I shouldn't have said it. It's just been a long trial. There were times it seemed like it was never going to end."

"Everything does, sometime."

Everything does.

"Look, maybe you and I need to go talk, get things settled," he said.

It had the sound of a close. Frannie sped up, suddenly desperate to get out of the room and into the open air and away from all the mistakes she'd made in her life. She shoved open the doors and strode out into the hall. And for the second time, came to an abrupt stop.

"Hello, Frances."

Cindy Fortune wore a demure black suit, probably a first for her. Next to her stood Josh, white-faced.

"Need some help?" a voice asked quietly behind her.

Frannie turned to see Roberto. He seemed so solid and reassuring, but this wasn't his fight. "I'm fine. Maybe…maybe you and Josh could go to the back doors and wait for me. This won't take long."

She watched for a minute to see them go and then turned back to Cindy. "What do you want, Mother?"

"The trial's over. I thought we could at least talk. Try to mend fences."

"Why would I want to talk to you?" Frannie asked. "You lied to me for nineteen years. Worse than lied. There aren't even words for what you did. You manipulated everyone."

"I don't want to fight," Cindy protested, "not over some stupid mistake I made a long time ago."

"You make it sound like you forgot to pack my lunch," Frannie said incredulously. "You stole from us, you stole our lives. Josh could have had a father who loved him, Roberto could have had a son. And they didn't, because you took that from them, you took it because in your twisted mind somehow it would benefit you."

"But I—"

"In your own way you're just as deluded as Lyndsey. She thought that whatever she did was okay as long as it gave her what she wanted. The end justified the means. Well, you know what, Mother? Some means can't be justified. What you did was unforgivable."

Cindy's defiance wobbled. "What do you want from me?"

"I want you to admit it. Just once I want to hear you take responsibility, to say 'I was wrong, I blew it, I screwed up. I wrecked your life and never lost a single night's sleep over it.'"

Cindy stared. "That's not true," she whispered. "Give me a chance."

"I gave you a chance," Frannie flared, "over and over again when I was a kid, every time you'd come back from disappearing, making promises about how wonderful everything was going to be. I always believed you because I couldn't imagine that you wouldn't be there if I just gave you one more chance. And every single time you broke my heart."

Frannie turned to walk away.

"Wait."

Frannie kept walking.

"Frannie stop, please."

Frannie turned around. "What?" she asked wearily.

"I was wrong." Cindy swallowed. "I screwed up. I thought I was… I thought of me," she said simply. She paused a long time. "There's no excuse, and the hell of it is, there's not a thing in the world I can do to fix it. All I can do is say I'm sorry and I'll be here for you, if you let me."

Frannie stared at her, feeling the familiar mix of emotions. Words had deserted her.

Cindy moistened her lips. "What can I do?"

"Right now? Leave it be for now. Go away for a while—you've always been good at that. Go to your friends in L.A. or London or wherever it is. Let some time go by." Frannie let out a long breath. "And maybe when you get back, we can try it all again."

"Are you relieved to have the trial over?" Roberto asked Josh.

They stood in the echoing marble hallway around the corner from the back doors of the building. Above them, the high ceiling threw down echoes. A few yards away were the closed doors of a courtroom; Roberto couldn't help wondering whose fate was being decided inside.

Like his fate was going to be decided now.

"Yeah," Josh said. "It's good to have it over."

"Good for everyone. Lyndsey included."

Josh bit his lip and focused on the floor. "You know, the hard thing was seeing her day after day, looking at me like it was all pretend, like we could go home and have pizza and laugh about it. But we're not going to laugh about it, are we?"

"I think you know the answer to that." Roberto studied Josh. The boy—man—had lost more weight over the course of the trial and his skin had turned sallow as he'd stayed inside to avoid the media. "Did you decide what you're doing about school?"

Josh shrugged. "I figure I'll take a couple years off. If I go to A&M now, people are going to be after me all the time with all the stuff about the trial. And there's the baby." He hesitated. "I was thinking maybe I'd volunteer for one of those charity groups that builds houses and schools and stuff. You know, do some good. Get the bad taste out of my mouth."

"This has been hell for you, hasn't it?" Roberto asked quietly.

"It's been kind of weird. It's like nothing's what I thought it was, not me and Lyndsey, not anything. My whole life I have a dad and now I find out he wasn't my dad after all."

Roberto was shaking his head before Josh even finished. "He was your dad, for better or worse. You had a life with him. Just because you don't have his blood doesn't negate it. There had to be some good times, some decent things he did. Remember that and let all the other stuff go."

"Yeah." Josh watched him. "So what happens with you and me?"

The $64,000 question that he'd been wrestling with for three months. When he wasn't wrestling with himself to keep from jumping on a plane and coming to find Frannie. "I guess that depends on you. I know what I want. I'd like to get a chance to know you. I'd like for you to get a chance to know me and my family. They're a good bunch of people."

"That so?"

Roberto nodded. "The first thing you should know is that no matter what, even if we never talk again, if you ever need anything, all you have to do is call. That goes for me or anyone in my family. Although I have to warn you, if you call and my mother answers, you're liable as not to get a lecture, depending on why you're calling."

Josh's lips twitched. "So, it's kind of like Mendoza AAA? With a twenty-four-hour hotline I can call?"

Roberto grinned. "Something like that. You'll be getting your membership card in the mail. It's also good for dinner on the house any time you want to stop by Red. Of course, I should also warn you that as a member of the family, any time you stop by Red you also run the risk of being press-ganged into busing tables."

"Live by the fajitas, die by the fajitas?"

Roberto clapped a hand on Josh's shoulder. "I thought you should know." He hesitated. "There's something else I wanted to talk to you about."

"Shoot."

"It's got to do with your mom." And it was all he'd been able to think about.

"She's been pretty quiet since you went back to Denver." Josh studied him. "You planning to do anything about that?"

"That depends on what she decides she wants."

"Yeah? What do you want?"

Roberto met his gaze. "I want your blessing. I've loved your mom for a long time. I guess maybe you know that. I'm a pretty traditional guy. Normally, I'd talk to her parents, but she hasn't got any worth speaking of. I figure you're her people now."

"You going to ask her to marry you?"

"That depends on her. You're not the only one who's been through the mill. I figure I'll ask something and if she says no, ask something else, and just keep on asking until I find a question she says yes to. After that, I'll just work my way up the ladder over time."

Josh thought about it for a minute, pursing his lips. "That's cool."

"Yeah?" Roberto asked.

Josh grinned. "Yeah."

"Good."

Down the hall, they heard the tapping of heels and saw Frannie heading toward them. And Roberto felt something squeeze in his chest.

"Hey," Josh said, "you play basketball?"

Roberto blinked. "Yeah, a little pickup. I've got a half court in my construction yard. Sometimes on Fridays some of the guys and I have a few beers and shoot some hoops. Why?"

"Stop by the house next time you're in the neighborhood. We can play a little one-on-one."

"Yeah?"

"Yeah."

Frannie came to a stop in front of them. "What are you two grinning about?"

"Basketball," Roberto said. "We're talking about basketball."

"How did your conversation with your mother go?" Roberto asked as they drove down the highway.

He'd suggested coffee, Frannie thought, but they'd breezed through Main Street and out into the open land beyond Red Rock.

She clasped her hands together. "It was good, I guess."

"You don't sound convinced."

"It was just different. Life with Cindy usually is. I said some things that were a long time coming. Nothing's fixed, but who knows, maybe things will be better.

In a way, I just feel better for having said it." She looked at him. "Does that make any kind of sense at all?"

"Sometimes just saying the words makes all the difference."

How could he understand her so well and yet be so far from her? "You and Josh seemed to be getting along all right."

"I think so. We'll see. He's a grown guy. He doesn't need someone coming in and suddenly trying to be his dad. I'd like to just be his friend."

"Did you tell him that?"

"In between talking about basketball."

Silence fell. Once, they'd been able to talk effortlessly. Now, despite everything that lay between them, she couldn't come up with anything to say.

Because the only things on her mind mattered too much.

Instead, she looked at the surrounding landscape. The afternoon was clear and warm, the way it had been weeks before when they'd lain beneath the oaks.

"I've always loved the hills this time of day," Roberto said, watching the highway carefully. He slowed and pulled off on a side road.

Frannie started. "Where on earth are you going? You said coffee."

"I know." He drummed his fingers on the steering wheel. "I just felt like being outdoors for a little bit after being stuck in that courtroom."

All around them were grassy slopes and trees. They bumped down through the ford of a stream bed and back out to the open field on the other side. Just beyond that, the road rose and rose farther until they came out on the crown of a hill. Roberto pulled the truck to a stop and turned off the engine.

"You're going to feel funny if whoever owns this place comes along and boots you out for trespassing," Frannie said as they got out.

"Relax, I know the guy who owns it."

She could hear the rustle of some burrowing creature in the grass. In the distance sounded the shrill piping calls of a killdeer. On the horizon, the sun blazed out, turning everything to copper. Roberto walked around to the back and lowered the tailgate so that they could sit.

Get things settled, he'd said. But he wasn't saying anything. Frannie tried to ignore the roiling in her stomach. "What a beautiful view. I don't think you could ever get tired of this," she said. And saw him tense. Something sank in her stomach. "I mean, just the hill country. I've always loved it out here."

She shifted to move away, but he caught her hand. "Yeah? You could maybe get used to this?"

Frannie moistened her lips. "What are you asking?"

"See that stake over there?" He pointed. "This property is mine. I closed on it yesterday morning. Six hundred some-odd acres, a couple of creeks and a natural aquifer that'll supply good, sweet well water. We can run some cattle, grow alfalfa, maybe raise horses."

"We?"

He took her hands in his. "We, Frannie. So what if we lost eighteen years? I don't give a damn. I spent every second of them missing you."

Her heart hammered. "But what about Colorado? You have a life there, a business. A home."

"My home is where you are," he said simply. "I was

gone for so long because I was closing up my business. And because I wanted to give you space. The night all hell broke loose, you told me I wasn't listening, that I was pushing too hard. I thought about that in the hospital. I thought about that a lot. And I realized you were right. And I figured the best thing I could do was just walk away, leave you alone so you could work things out."

Her throat tightened. "You just disappeared."

"If I'd come to you again, I never would have left. I couldn't have. And I needed to, for you and for me, both. I needed to make myself give you the space. You need to get comfortable with your life. And I realize you may not be there yet, but I've got enough work to do here to keep me busy for a good long time. Not too busy to miss you, but love also means patience, and I do love you, Frannie, I do. I always have."

He put a hand to her cheek. "I'm sorry that somehow got mixed up so you didn't feel like I was giving you what you needed. Just take your time, build your empires, do what you need to do, but I'll be here. And if you could see your way clear to letting me be at your side while you're doing your empire building, you'd make me a really happy man."

She threw her arms around him and pressed her face to his neck. "Oh, Roberto, I love you so much. I've always known it, but the second Lyndsey pointed that gun at you, all I could think was that I'd been a fool to ever push you away. And then you disappeared and I thought you were gone forever."

"I'm never going to be gone again. I'll always be at your side. I want to marry you and make you happy. I want to get back everything we missed out on, and if we can have more kids, what the hell, let's do it."

The light turned to gold as the sun hit the horizon—the magic hour.

Frannie cradled his face in her hands. "Roberto, I love you. There's nothing I want more in the world than to spend the rest of my life with you."

"Then what are we waiting for?" He kissed her.

And in that magic hour, they sank to the grass as one.

Epilogue

Torches flickered above the masses of blackfoot daisies and purple sage in the gardens of the Double Crown. Fairy lights twinkled in the cedar elms. Music drifted through the air. It was a night for magic, for promises. Silk and white roses, the time-honored words: to have, to hold, to love, to cherish, forsaking all others, from this day forward.

It was magic and moonlight and Roberto drew Frannie away to a small path that wound among the honey mesquite.

"Our guests," Frannie protested.

"They'll have you for the rest of the night." He leaned in to press his lips to the shadowed hollow above her collar bone. "I only want five minutes alone with my wife."

Frannie shivered. "Tell me it's real," she murmured.

"It's real." He wrapped an arm around her waist and

swept her close to him for a lingering kiss. "But I'll be happy to prove it to you every day for the rest of my life."

"Mmm. Every day?" she murmured against his lips.

"Maybe every other day. I am pushing forty, you know."

She laughed. "You're so decrepit."

"Remember, you said in sickness and in health. I have witnesses." He pointed across the gardens to where the reception was being held.

Old friends and new, the two families together again, this time tied by an even stronger bond. Frannie felt a bubble of joy swell in her chest. "Come on, let's go walk around and talk with those witnesses."

"As long as you promise I get you to myself tonight."

She gave him a smacking kiss. "I promise you get me to yourself for life."

"Hey, no hiding out there alone all night, you two," scolded Maria Mendoza as they walked back to the reception area. She and José were at the edge of the dance floor, swaying to the sounds of Ol' Blue Eyes singing "All of Me." Beyond, Lily and William Sr. danced together as he held her hand his against his chest.

Roberto bowed to Frannie. "Would you like to dance, Mrs. Mendoza?"

"I'd be delighted, Mr. Mendoza."

She'd never been happier, Frannie thought as she stepped into his arms. Across the floor her brother Ross danced with his girlfriend Julie Osterman, and nearer, Isabella and J.R. laughed as they tried to practice the foxtrot with Jane and Jorge. Dress rehearsal for their own wedding in just a few weeks, no doubt.

And at a table nearby, Frannie saw her firefighter cousin, Darr, making faces at a tiny girl in a frilly white dress, his dark blond hair mixing with her golden curls. His beautiful wife, Bethany, sat beside them, smiling.

"Oh, let's go say hello," Frannie begged, tugging Roberto over to their table. "Hey, Darr, got a hot date?"

"Bethany was playing hard to get," he said, bouncing his four-month-old daughter on his knee.

"Bethany's strictly B-list these days," his wife corrected, but the expression in her eyes was fond.

"Miranda, meet Auntie Frannie and Uncle Roberto. Can you say auntie, smart girl?" Darr asked.

Miranda burbled obligingly and stared raptly up at them with her cornflower-blue eyes.

"She's beautiful, Bethany."

"Did you hear that, Randi? She called you beautiful," Darr cooed.

Frannie laughed. "I think someone might have Daddy wrapped around her little finger."

Bethany's lips twitched. "I shudder to think how it's going to be once she starts dating."

"It'll be fine, Randi, won't it?" Darr said. "Because it won't happen until you're thirty, will it?" He tickled her chin until she giggled delightedly.

"They look happy," Roberto commented as they wandered away, drifting back toward the gardens.

"If you like babies, just wait a couple of months, we'll have them coming out of our ears," Frannie said. "Darr and Bethany's, Josh's, Nick and Charlene's—" she nodded to her cousin's now very pregnant wife "—and ours."

"Good babysitting practice for when—" He stopped and stared at her. "Did you just say what I thought you said?"

Frannie nodded, watching his expression morph from surprise to joy.

He picked her up and whirled her around. "Tell me it's real," he demanded.

"It's real," she laughed.

"We're going to have a baby? When?"

"About six and a half months. I think it happened that night you took me out to show me your ranch. I guess that property's good luck."

"You're good luck," he murmured, pressing a kiss on her. "After all, you're my fortune."

* * * * *

*Celebrate 60 years of pure reading
pleasure with Harlequin®!*

*Harlequin Presents® is proud to introduce
its gripping new miniseries,*
THE ROYAL HOUSE OF KAREDES.
*An exquisite coronation diamond, split as a symbol of
a warring royal family's feud, is missing! But
whoever reunites the diamond halves will rule all....*

*Welcome to eight brand-new titles that unfold to
reveal the stories of kings and queens, princes and
princesses torn apart by pride and power, but finally
reunited by love.*

Step into the world of Karedes with
BILLIONAIRE PRINCE, PREGNANT MISTRESS
Available July 2009 from Harlequin Presents®.

ALEXANDROS KAREDES, SNOW DUSTING the shoulders of his leather jacket and glittering like jewels in his dark hair, stood at the door. Maria felt the blood drain from her head.

"Good evening, Ms. Santos."

His voice was as she remembered it. Deep. Husky. Perfect English, but with the faintest hint of a Greek accent. And cold, as cold as it had been that awful morning she would never forget, when he'd accused her of horrible things, called her terrible names....

"Aren't you going to ask me in?"

She fought for composure. Last time they'd faced each other, they'd been on his turf. Now they were on hers. She was in command here, and that meant everything.

"There's a sign on the door downstairs," she said, her tone every bit as frigid as his. "It says, 'No soliciting or vagrants.'"

His lips drew back in a wolfish grin. "Very amusing."

"What do you want, Prince Alexandros?"

A tight smile eased across his mouth and it killed her that even now, knowing he was a vicious, arrogant man, she couldn't help but notice what a handsome mouth it was. Chiseled. Generous. Beautiful, like the rest of him, which made him living proof that beauty could, indeed, be only skin deep.

"Such formality, Maria. You were hardly so proper the last time we were together."

She knew his choice of words was deliberate. She felt her face heat; she couldn't help that but she damned well didn't have to let him lure her into a verbal sparring match.

"I'll ask you once more, Your Highness. What do you want?"

"Ask me in and I'll tell you."

"I have no intention of asking you in. Tell me why you're here or don't. It's your choice, just as it will be my choice to shut the door in your face."

He laughed. It infuriated her but she could hardly blame him. He was tall—six two, six three—and though he stood with one shoulder leaning against the door frame, hands tucked casually into the pockets of the jacket, his pose was deceptive. He was strong, with the leanly muscled body of a well-trained athlete.

She remembered his body with painful clarity. The

feel of him under her hands. The power of him moving over her. The taste of him on her tongue.

Suddenly, he straightened, his laughter gone. "I have not come this distance to stand in your doorway," he said coldly, "and I am not going to leave until I am ready to do so. I suggest you stand aside and stop behaving like a petulant child."

A petulant child? Was that what he thought? This man who had spent hours making love to her and had then accused her of—of trading her body for profit?

Except it had not been love, it had been sex. And the sooner she got rid of him, the better.

She let go of the doorknob and stepped aside. "You have five minutes."

He strolled past her, bringing cold air and the scent of the night with him. She swung toward him, arms folded. He reached past her, pushed the door closed, then folded his arms, too. She wanted to open the door again but she'd be damned if she was going to get into a who's-in-charge-here argument with him. She was in charge, and he would surely see a tussle over the ground rules as a sign of weakness.

Instead, she looked past him at the big clock above her work table.

"Ten seconds gone," she said briskly. "You're wasting time, Your Highness."

"What I have to say will take longer than five minutes."

"Then you'll just have to learn to economize. More than five minutes, I'll call the police."

Instantly, his hand was wrapped around her wrist. He

tugged her toward him, his dark-chocolate eyes almost black with anger.

"You do that and I'll tell every tabloid shark I can contact about how Maria Santos tried to buy a five-hundred-thousand-dollar commission by seducing a prince." He smiled thinly. "They'll lap it up."

* * * * *

What will it take for this billionaire prince to realize he's falling in love with his mistress…?
Look for
BILLIONAIRE PRINCE, PREGNANT MISTRESS
by Sandra Marton
Available July 2009 from Harlequin Presents®.

We'll be spotlighting a different series every month throughout 2009 to celebrate our 60th anniversary.

Look for Harlequin® Presents in July!

TWO CROWNS, TWO ISLANDS, ONE LEGACY

A royal family, torn apart by pride and its lust for power, reunited by purity and passion

Step into the world of Karedes beginning this July with

BILLIONAIRE PRINCE, PREGNANT MISTRESS

by

Sandra Marton

Eight volumes to collect and treasure!

From *New York Times*
bestselling authors

CARLA NEGGERS

SUSAN MALLERY
KAREN HARPER

More Than Words:
STORIES OF
STRENGTH

They're your neighbors, your aunts, your sisters and your best friends. They're women across North America committed to changing and enriching lives, one good deed at a time. Three of these exceptional women have been selected as recipients of Harlequin's More Than Words award. And three *New York Times* bestselling authors have kindly offered their creativity to write original short stories inspired by these real-life heroines.

Visit **www.HarlequinMoreThanWords.com**
to find out more, or to nominate
a real-life heroine in your life.

**Proceeds from the sale of this book will be
reinvested in Harlequin's charitable initiatives.**

Available in March 2009 wherever books are sold.

INTRODUCING THE FIFTH ANNUAL
MORE THAN WORDS ANTHOLOGY

Five bestselling authors
Five real-life heroines

A little comfort, caring and compassion go a long way toward making the world a better place. Just ask the dedicated women handpicked from countless worthy nominees across North America to become this year's recipients of Harlequin's More Than Words award. To celebrate their accomplishments, five bestselling authors have honored the winners by writing short stories inspired by these real-life heroines.

New stories inspired by real women who've changed lives

HEATHER GRAHAM

NEW YORK TIMES BESTSELLING AUTHOR

More Than Words
VOLUME 5

CANDACE CAMP
STEPHANIE BOND
BRENDA JACKSON
TARA TAYLOR QUINN

Visit **www.HarlequinMoreThanWords.com**
to find out more, or to nominate
a real-life heroine in your life.

**Proceeds from the sale of this book will be
reinvested in Harlequin's charitable initiatives.**

Available in April 2009 wherever books are sold.

THE BELLES OF TEXAS

They're as strong as the state that raised
them. The Belle sisters aren't afraid to go
after what they want, whether it's reclaiming
their ranch or their family.

Linda Warren
CAITLYN'S PRIZE

Thanks to her deceased father's gambling
debts, Caitlyn Belle's beloved High Five Ranch
is in dire straits. Particularly because the
will stipulates that if the ranch doesn't turn
a profit in six months, it must be sold to
Judd Calhoun—the man Caitlyn jilted
fourteen years ago. And Cait knows Judd has
been waiting a long time for his revenge....

*Look for the first book
in The Belles of Texas miniseries,
on sale in July wherever books are sold.*

You're invited to join our Tell Harlequin Reader Panel!

By joining our new reader panel you will:

- Receive Harlequin® books—they are FREE and yours to keep with no obligation to purchase anything!
- Participate in fun online surveys
- Exchange opinions and ideas with women just like you
- Have a say in our new book ideas and help us publish the best in women's fiction

In addition, you will have a chance to win great prizes and receive special gifts! See Web site for details. Some conditions apply. Space is limited.

To join, visit us at
www.TellHarlequin.com.

REQUEST YOUR FREE BOOKS!

2 FREE NOVELS PLUS 2 FREE GIFTS!

SPECIAL EDITION®

Life, Love and Family!

YES! Please send me 2 FREE Silhouette Special Edition® novels and my 2 FREE gifts (gifts are worth about $10). After receiving them, if I don't wish to receive any more books, I can return the shipping statement marked "cancel." If I don't cancel, I will receive 6 brand-new novels every month and be billed just $4.24 per book in the U.S. or $4.99 per book in Canada. That's a savings of at least 15% off the cover price! It's quite a bargain! Shipping and handling is just 50¢ per book.* I understand that accepting the 2 free books and gifts places me under no obligation to buy anything. I can always return a shipment and cancel at any time. Even if I never buy another book from Silhouette, the two free books and gifts are mine to keep forever.

235 SDN EYN4   335 SDN EYPG

Name	(PLEASE PRINT)	
Address		Apt. #
City	State/Prov.	Zip/Postal Code

Signature (if under 18, a parent or guardian must sign)

Mail to the **Silhouette Reader Service:**
IN U.S.A.: P.O. Box 1867, Buffalo, NY 14240-1867
IN CANADA: P.O. Box 609, Fort Erie, Ontario L2A 5X3

Not valid to current subscribers of Silhouette Special Edition books.

Want to try two free books from another line?
Call 1-800-873-8635 or visit www.morefreebooks.com.

* Terms and prices subject to change without notice. Prices do not include applicable taxes. Sales tax applicable in N.Y. Canadian residents will be charged applicable provincial taxes and GST. Offer not valid in Quebec. This offer is limited to one order per household. All orders subject to approval. Credit or debit balances in a customer's account(s) may be offset by any other outstanding balance owed by or to the customer. Please allow 4 to 6 weeks for delivery. Offer available while quantities last.

Your Privacy: Silhouette is committed to protecting your privacy. Our Privacy Policy is available online at www.eHarlequin.com or upon request from the Reader Service. From time to time we make our lists of customers available to reputable third parties who may have a product or service of interest to you. If you would prefer we not share your name and address, please check here. ☐

SSE09R

Stay up-to-date on all your romance reading news!

The Inside Romance newsletter is a **FREE** quarterly newsletter highlighting our upcoming series releases and promotions!

Go to

eHarlequin.com/InsideRomance

or e-mail us at

InsideRomance@Harlequin.com

to sign up to receive

your **FREE** newsletter today!

You can also subscribe by writing to us at: HARLEQUIN BOOKS
Attention: Customer Service Department
P.O. Box 9057, Buffalo, NY 14269-9057

Please allow 4-6 weeks for delivery of the first issue by mail.

IRN-NBPAO109

Silhouette®

COMING NEXT MONTH

Available June 30, 2009

#1981 THE TEXAS BILLIONAIRE'S BRIDE—Crystal Green
The Foleys and the McCords
For Vegas showgirl turned nanny Melanie Grandy, caring for the daughter of gruff billionaire Zane Foley was the perfect gig…until she fell for him, and her secret past threatened to bring down the curtain on her newfound happiness.

#1982 THE DOCTOR'S SECRET BABY—Teresa Southwick
Men of Mercy Medical
It was no secret that Emily Summers had shared a night of passion with commitment-phobe Dr. Cal Westen. But she kept him in the dark when she had their child. Would a crisis bring them together as a family…for good?

#1983 THE 39-YEAR-OLD VIRGIN—Marie Ferrarella
It wasn't easy when Claire Santaniello had to leave the convent to teach and take care of her sick mother. Luckily, widowed father and vice detective Caleb McClain was there for her as she found her way in the world…and into his arms.

#1984 HIS BROTHER'S BRIDE-TO-BE—Patricia Kay
Jill Jordan Emerson was engaged to a wealthy businessman several years her senior—until she came face-to-face with his younger brother Stephen Wells, a.k.a. the long-lost father of her son! Now which brother would claim this bride-to-be as his own?

#1985 LONE STAR DADDY—Stella Bagwell
Men of the West
It was a simple case of illegal cattle trafficking on a New Mexico ranch, and Ranger Jonas Redman thought he had the assignment under control—until the ranch's very single, very pregnant heiress Alexa Cantrell captured his attention and wouldn't let go….

#1986 YOUR RANCH OR MINE?—Cindy Kirk
Meet Me in Montana
When designer Anna Anderssen came home to Sweet River, she should have known she'd run right into neighboring rancher Mitchell Donovan, the one man who could expose the secrets—and reignite passions—that made her run in the first place!

SSECNMBPA0609